THE BOY-FREE ZONE

Veronica Bennett works part-time as an English lecturer. She began her writing career as a freelance journalist, but soon moved into fiction. Her first book, *Monkey*, was published in 1998 and was acclaimed by *The Times Educational Supplement* as "an impressively well-written and audacious debut". She has since written *Dandelion and Bobcat*, and for older readers, *Fish Feet*. Veronica Bennett is married to a university professor and has two children.

GW00778991

Books by the same author

Dandelion and Bobcat
Fish Feet
Monkey

THE
BOY-FREE
ZONE

VERONICA BENNETT

WALKER BOOKS
AND SUBSIDIARIES
LONDON • BOSTON • SYDNEY

First published 1999 by Walker Books Ltd
87 Vauxhall Walk, London SE11 5HJ

This edition published 2002

2 4 6 8 10 9 7 5 3

Quote on page 108 is from *Mrs Dalloway*, by Virginia Woolf

This book has been typeset in Sabon

Printed in Great Britain by Cox & Wyman Ltd, Reading, Berkshire

British Library Cataloguing in Publication Data:
a catalogue record for this book is
available from the British Library

ISBN 0-7445-9046-9

For Lynda Pitt
Artist

CONTENTS

Part Three: The Glass Gazebo

PART ONE
The Silver Tunnel

GARGOYLES

Annabel's bottom hurt. The top of the wall was narrow, and very hard. She shifted her weight onto her left buttock, rubbing the other one. "Are you sure about this, Lucy?"

"He'll come," promised Lucy, scanning the tennis courts. "Laura told me."

"You mean you trust what Laura says? I wouldn't—"

"There he is!" Lucy clutched Annabel's arm so suddenly, and so tightly, that they both almost overbalanced.

"Lucy, be careful! Sudden death isn't necessary, you know, even for Sean Turnbull."

"Shut up and *look*!"

Annabel looked. Laura Turnbull's brother Scan and a middle-aged man came out of the clubhouse wearing sweaters and swinging their racquets. Sean's smooth, bony legs came out of his shorts, ending in thick white socks

11

and trainers with tabs at the back. He went to his end of the court, the evening sun making a long shadow behind him, and began to jog from foot to foot and crouch down like tennis players on TV. The man served a ball, which Sean missed.

Lucy giggled. "Go on, Sean, try hitting the ball *over* the net!"

Annabel's heart climbed up and settled somewhere north of her ribcage. Sean, who would be seventeen on Wednesday, exactly six months and three days after she had turned fifteen, was doing a lot of running about, reaching for the balls his father was hitting to him. His hair flopped about in the sunlight as he bent to pick them up and stuff them into the pocket of his shorts. She watched him practise serving, throwing balls up and swiping them. His arm made an artistic arc in the air. He wasn't a very tall boy – probably not much taller than Lucy, who was tall for a girl, but he looked all right. And given the circumstances, the fact that he existed at all was nothing short of miraculous.

"Come on, Turnbull, off with that sweater!" urged Lucy breathlessly. "Let's see whether your shirt's in or out!"

Lucy and Annabel had laid bets on this before, and on whether or not he would be leaning against the bus stop when they passed each morning on the way to school. It wasn't a very exciting game, but in Broughton you had to make your own entertainment.

At that moment he put his racquet between his knees and grasped the neck of the sweater. Annabel gave a muted shriek. Sean and his father turned, saw the two girls sitting on the wall and exchanged looks. Annabel ducked her head. How embarrassing. This business with Sean Turnbull was getting out of hand.

"Let's go," she suggested, feeling hot. "It's getting late. And my bum hurts."

"But he's only just come out. And you're the one who's always going on about him."

"Only because there's no one else to go on about."

Lucy's eyes narrowed. "Do you mean I've had to tolerate that dopey Laura all this time for nothing?"

"I'm sorry, Lucy." Annabel took one last look. "But I just think I'm going off him."

"Oh, great." Lucy swung her legs over the wall and slid to the ground. "So who's next for the treatment? Dennis in the hardware shop? Those two old blokes who sit outside the pub all day? At least they're male, I suppose."

Annabel's legs were shorter than Lucy's. She couldn't get off the wall.

"Here," said Lucy crossly. "Hold on to me."

Annabel's feet hurt when she jumped onto them. She stamped them, and rubbed the

13

backs of her legs. "I'm never doing that again, not for Sean Turnbull or anyone else."

"As if there *were* anyone else," muttered Lucy.

It had been the last day of term. The summer stretched ahead like a magic carpet. Empty, waiting for Annabel to step onto it. When Lucy had suggested they change out of their uniforms and spy on Sean Turnbull's game, Annabel had agreed without hesitation. She had no desire to hasten the moment when her mother would open the brown envelope with the school crest in the corner. Being pretty isn't enough, Annabel, she'd say. You lazy little toad, you haven't done a damn thing this term, have you?

Before she'd left the house Annabel had hidden the report behind the framed photograph of herself as a three-year-old, winning the Miss Baby Scarborough competition. Her mother would have to find it for herself.

They dawdled along the deserted High Street. Annabel wondered if Lucy was thinking about her own report, which was bound to be excellent though she made so little effort at school. It was depressing that so many subjects came easily to Lucy, but it was even more depressing that none of them came easily to Annabel. Except possibly Art, which she liked. Art wasn't much use, though. And next year there would be exams.

At the corner of Lucy's street they stopped beside the telephone box. The glass reflected their identical blue jeans, identical shoes and identical socks turned over at exactly the same place. Identical blue and white checked tops, too, bought at the same shop on the same day. Lucy was dark, but Annabel's fine gold hair and blue eyes had long ago earned her the nickname "Barbie-Brain". She hated it, but was reluctantly grateful to Lucy for thinking of it. At least it made people remember who Annabel Bairstow was, which was an advantage in a girls' school as huge and impersonal as Hilda Greenaway McDowd.

"I know what Broughton is," said Lucy, her eyes shining with inspiration. "It's a Boy-free Zone! You know, like they declare places a Nuclear-free Zone or a Litter-free Zone. My mum's on the Parish Council. I'll speak to her about it."

"Oh, Lucy, don't." Annabel had realized it was a joke. "But you're right. It's stupid, having separate schools twenty miles apart."

The closure of Broughton Boys' school meant that every boy in a twenty-mile radius had to be bussed to Horwell, and every girl to Hilda Greenaway McDowd. Poor Hilda must be turning in her grave, thought Annabel.

"The trouble is," said Lucy, leaning restlessly against the telephone box, "everyone in Broughton already knows everyone else. So what chance have we got of meeting anyone new? Especially new *boys*?"

The church clock began to strike half-past seven. "There *are* some boys, you know," said Annabel. "Of the right age, and everything."

"Name one. *Not* Sean Turnbull."

"Well, what about the boys who were in our year at Broughton Juniors?"

Lucy looked exasperated. "Do me a favour, Annabel. And there were only six of them, anyway."

"Well – Dennis in the hardware store, then," suggested Annabel. "Laura says he's saving up for a motorbike."

Lucy looked doubtful. But Annabel struggled on. "And we've met some Horwell boys, haven't we? I know they weren't up to much, but—"

"Look, Annabel," said Lucy patiently, "Horwell's seventeen miles away. If more boys had cars, or even motorbikes, that would be fine. But I'm not prepared to spend hours every day on that smelly old bus just for the privilege of going out with a Horwell boy, even if you are."

Annabel was beginning to feel discouraged. "I'm sure there are lots of boys around, Lucy. It's just that they're – well–"

"*Gargoyles,*" supplied Lucy glumly, pushing her hair behind her ears.

Annabel watched her friend's face, which

was pink under the gold tint it always acquired at the first touch of the sun. She admired it without envy. Lucy wasn't as pretty as she was – everyone knew that – but Annabel always liked looking at her.

"I must go home," she said. "Really. It's very late."

Lucy nodded. "Do you think Sean's managed to hit the ball yet?"

"I don't know." Annabel set off up the hill. "I don't much care, anyway."

"But you were so keen on him!"

She stopped and turned. Lucy was standing on the corner, her shadow zig-zagging against the telephone box. The sun had almost gone. "I've just changed my mind, that's all."

"If you ask me," said Lucy, beginning a grin, "any Barbie-Brain worth her beach-disco outfit can do much better than him anyway. Let's go into Horwell tonight and see if any new talent's turned up, shall we?"

"Lucy, I can't."

"Why not? That boy who serves the ice-cream at Brown's keeps looking at you."

"Janet's having a party tonight. I've got to stay in and help her with it."

Lucy grimaced. She had experience of Annabel's mother's parties. "Not sausage rolls cut in half to make them go further? And cheese and pineapple chunks on sticks?"

"Probably."

"And *quiche*?"

"Definitely!"

They smiled sympathetically at each other.

"I'll come round in the morning and help you clear up the mess," said Lucy. "And we'll go into Horwell tomorrow night, shall we?"

"We always do, Luce."

Lucy's smile widened. "Well, you never know…" She turned to go. "See you tomorrow, then. Enjoy the party."

"As if!"

Annabel walked on up the hill. At the summit, she stopped by the cottage gate and looked down at Broughton. Only the very highest roofs were lit now, with a tired, yellowish light. The rest of the village lay in deep shadow.

This was the place where Annabel had been born, and her father and grandfather had been born too. But the ugly hilltop cottage wasn't the house she'd been born in. It was part of the big change in Annabel's life, and she wondered if she'd ever get used to living there.

The cottage was set so near the road it seemed to be waiting to cross it. Its walls, which were made of grey stone like everything else in Broughton, had resisted all Janet's attempts to train roses over them, and its square little casement windows glared at the passing cars. Annabel looked up at her bedroom in the roof above the porch, and sighed.

She thought about what Lucy had said about the Boy-free Zone.

It wasn't as if she wanted to go out with a different boy every night. All she asked for was one. Not Sean Turnbull, or the boy who served the ice-cream in Brown's, but someone she hadn't met yet. He didn't have to be what Lucy called "talent", and he didn't have to look like the boys who posed and pouted on the posters in girls' magazines. He just had to be – she swung the gate a couple of times, trying to think of the word – *nice*? It wasn't much of a word, but it was the best she could come up with.

Whoever he was, and wherever he was lurking, he just had to be nice enough for her to like, and to like her. Surely that wasn't too much to ask?

MISS PRUNEFACE

Norman, Annabel's elderly tortoiseshell cat, climbed into her lap as she sat down in the rocking chair. She tickled the back of his neck.

"You lazy old slug," she told him softly. "You've been dozing on that windowsill all afternoon, haven't you?"

Her mother came in carrying a large cardboard box, her lips pressed together in a line. She was wearing a shrunken T-shirt and the tie-dye skirt which always looked to Annabel as if she'd spilt something on it. Taking some wine glasses out of the box, she placed them haphazardly on the dresser. "Put that cat down and *help*, can't you?" she said to Annabel without looking at her.

Annabel wondered for the millionth time whose insane idea it was for mothers to be students. It was bad enough that Janet and Dad had split up after years of assuring Annabel they wouldn't, but even worse was that less than a month after Dad had moved out Janet had enrolled on a course in Women's Studies, whatever that was. And she wanted Annabel to call her Janet, not Mum, from now on.

"I don't want to be your mum any more," she'd explained, not very tactfully. "I want to be your Janet."

"Why?" Annabel had asked. She was only thirteen then.

"Because women fragment themselves, and I want to be whole again."

Baffled, Annabel had tried to accept the new Janet with good grace. But two years later, she wasn't sure if Janet knew *what* she wanted. Dad, whose patience with Janet survived even their estrangement, explained without bitterness that he and Annabel should support her metamorphosis from Mum to Person, and everything would turn out all right in the end. Despite his reassurances, though, Annabel always felt that she herself fitted into the new scheme of things awkwardly, like a jigsaw piece from the wrong puzzle.

She and Norman settled further into the uncushioned wooden chair. It wasn't very comfortable, but every other seat in the room was covered with party paraphernalia. A bag of balloons and the pump for blowing them up, unsteady piles of borrowed CDs, packets of paper serviettes.

"Look at all this stuff! I'll never get finished." Janet's gaze roved aimlessly over the chaos. "Do you think I could get away with not warming up the quiche?"

Annabel considered. "Well, cold quiche is even more disgusting than warm quiche, but I don't suppose your friends will even notice."

"Don't be spiteful, please."

"I'm not. I'm just stating a fact," said Annabel mildly.

"Hoity-toity," murmured Janet, beginning on another box of glasses.

Annabel began to be depressed. She watched Janet turning this way and that like a marionette, swinging her gold and silver hair, and wondered whether wishing you didn't have to live with your mother meant that you were a wicked person. Living with Dad in his little hutch of a house in Horwell had never been possible, because he was away on business so often, and there was no girls' school there anyway.

Annabel had been abandoned to Janet.

A week ago, Dad had moved to London. Janet had told Annabel, suddenly and without apology, that he'd been offered a partnership in a building firm there, and had already put his own business up for sale. "He thinks it's the best thing for all of us, darling," she'd said. "It'll give us a bit of space."

Annabel had protested, horrified, that she

didn't want *space*. The only space she wanted to be in was one which also contained Dad. Without the familiar, Dad-shaped scaffold to hold it up, life as Annabel knew it would fall down. Why didn't Janet realize that? Was it so impossible that she might occasionally understand *something* about her own daughter?

The worst thing, though, was that Dad wouldn't be there to help Annabel with the only thing she was interested in. She could scarcely believe he had forsaken their Saturday morning painting lessons for a job opportunity, however golden. After he'd driven away in his little green van with ALAN BAIRSTOW DESIGN AND BUILD on the side she'd hidden in her bedroom and cried. But Janet, whose small store of sympathy was soon exhausted, had told her briskly that if Dad wanted to start again somewhere else, that was that. Annabel would just have to accept that she couldn't always have her own way.

Janet breathed on a glass and rubbed it on her skirt. "Would you blow up some balloons, baby?"

"Why should I blow up balloons for a party I don't want to go to?"

Janet stopped polishing and looked at her with disapproval. "What's the matter with you, Miss Pruneface? When I was fifteen I'd have *died* for the chance to go to a party like this."

23

"I wish you *were* fifteen," said Annabel sulkily. "Then I wouldn't be born and you wouldn't have to worry about how boring I am."

"Oh, shut up." Janet started to rub the glass again. "If you're spoiling for a fight, I'm not going to give you one. I'm going to offer non-violent resistance, like Mahatma Gandhi."

Annabel tried to think of any quality her mother could possibly have in common with Gandhi. Or Martin Luther King, or Nelson Mandela or any of the other peace icons she was always holding up for Annabel to worship. "You're not interested in me," she said. This was a truth she'd wanted to voice for ages. "You're not interested in anything I do."

"Rubbish!" Non-violent resistance had been abandoned. Janet's eyes, which were as blue as Annabel's, looked extra blue. She leaned forward, exposing a cushiony cleavage and a strip of petticoat lace. "*You're* the one who's not interested in anything. If you're boring, that's not *my* fault, is it?"

Annabel thought about the report behind the photograph on the mantelpiece. She thought about watching Sean Turnbull from the wall, which had made her feel grubby and secretive. She thought about the way Janet, who always said that people should just *be*, never missed a chance to remind her daughter that she hadn't turned out the way she wanted.

"I *am* boring," she said calmly. "How can you stand to be in the room with such a boring person?"

Janet stared at her for a moment. Then she sat down on the arm of the rocking chair. Norman blinked warily and padded away. Janet's musky perfume made Annabel's nose itch. She shifted, trying not to breathe.

"What's the matter, sweetheart?" Janet's face looked troubled. "I hardly know what to make of you these days. You used to be such a co-operative little girl."

"When I had two parents, you mean?"

Janet sighed, and reached for the balloon pump. "Look, baby girl, why don't you blow up the balloons while I set the food out on the kitchen table? And after that, I know what we'll do! Let's make each other look gorgeous, like we used to!"

Annabel heard the plaintiveness in her mother's voice. But how could Janet expect her to be the little girl she longed for – the "baby" she was always calling her – when each day pushed childhood deeper into the past?

She looked at Janet's round, soft-cheeked face, displaying eagerness and dread in about equal measure, and gave in. She took the balloon pump. "All right." Then a thought struck her. "Are there going to be students – young ones, I mean – at the party?"

25

Janet stood up and shook the creases out of her skirt. "Yes, of course. Now, I must get on. Frank's coming round in a minute. Is that pump working all right?"

Annabel nodded. "Can I invite Lucy?"

Janet's shoulders stiffened. "Don't be pathetic, Annabel."

"But you just said that when you were fifteen you'd have *died*—"

"Shut up and make a start on those balloons. I'll be in the kitchen if you want me."

So much for Gandhi, then.

Despair propelled Annabel out of the chair. She picked up the bag of balloons and went outside. Dusk was falling, but in the shadowy garden it was still very warm. Annabel sat down on the low wall between the garden and the field behind the cottage. The smells of grass and evening-scented stock mingled in the air, which felt stormy. As usual, now the holidays had started, the best of the summer was over.

"Getting a breath of air, lass? I don't blame you – it's hotter than a works' furnace in that kitchen."

Annabel looked up unwillingly. Then she looked down again at the bag in her hand. "Hello, Mr Houseman."

"Hello, Miss Bairstow."

Frank Houseman was the owner of Houseman's Feed and Seed, the agricultural merchants

26

in the High Street. He lived alone a mile or so away at Cairncross, an old farm on the main road to Horwell which had no animals and grew nothing but grass. Lately he had taken to calling in at the cottage on his way home from work. Annabel, upstairs doing her homework, would hear his resonant voice and Janet's gurgling laughter from the kitchen.

It had crossed Annabel's mind that he was lonely, but this didn't make her eager to be friendly towards him. In his presence she often felt awkward, though it was difficult to work out whether the awkwardness came from him or her. And even though he'd been at the closed-down boys' school with her father, if he passed her in the street there was only half a chance that he would acknowledge her.

He sat beside her uninvited. There was a can of beer in his hand. "Looking forward to the party?"

She flicked him a tiny look, noticing for the first time how abnormally hairy his arms were. They came out of his short sleeves like a chimpanzee's arms. The light from the tree-lanterns he'd helped Janet rig up yesterday shone on two bald patches above his temples. "No, not much," she said.

"Oh dear." He shifted his weight, crossing his legs. Annabel saw that he was wearing beige-coloured shoes, with blue socks which didn't match them. "None of Janet's long-haired lot to your liking, eh?"

He watched her for a moment from under untidy eyebrows. Then he took a sip of beer and put the can down on the wall. "I had a bit of a chat with Alan recently," he announced. Alan was Annabel's father. "He came into my yard for summat or other. We weren't busy, so I sat in the shop and talked to him. He told me about his new firm. And he talked a bit about you, too."

The way he said "summat or other" grated on Annabel's nerves. He only used Yorkshire dialect because he thought it made him sound like a self-made man, which he wasn't. Everyone knew that he had inherited both Cairncross and the feed business from his father, and had been to college in America. Dad, who was also a farmer's son, but without the benefit of such privileges, was the one with the authentic accent.

"I hope he said something nice," she said quietly.

"He tells me you're keen on drawing. Is that right?"

Suspicion tugged at Annabel's heart. Why should a man who hardly knew her discuss this with her father? And she wished he hadn't used that loathsome parent-word, *keen*.

"You like Art at school, do you?" he asked.

"It's OK."

He stroked his moustache. "Only OK?"

28

"Well..." She tried to work out why he wanted to know and what she was prepared to tell him. "At school they just make you draw the same things over and over again. It's so tedious." Especially, she might have added, since it was Dad who made it interesting and fun, and he couldn't do that from two hundred miles away.

"But if you're good at it," he persisted, "it's worth carrying on with, isn't it? Alan thinks so."

Annabel's sulk intensified. She couldn't tell him how impossible it was to get anyone to take her interest in art seriously. Mr Lefevre was a good teacher, but had to divide his time between too many girls. And Dad's instruction, though helpful, had always been erratic. She needed a constant supply of art materials, too, which she hated nagging him for. Above all, she needed fellow enthusiasts, who wouldn't scoff at what she was trying to do.

"I'm not particularly good at it, Mr Houseman," she said, her voice still very small.

"Call me Frank, lass." His vowels were flatter than Dad's, with harder edges. He took another sip of beer. "I'm sure it would please Alan if you bothered with your drawing. And Janet, too, of course."

Annabel took a balloon out of the bag and began, half-heartedly, to blow it up. "I don't care what Janet thinks," she said.

"Oh." He ran his hand over his chin. "Well, it was just a thought."

Lucy had once told Annabel that the best way to unsettle an adult was to be extra polite, and call them Mr or Mrs even when they'd given you permission not to. They didn't expect it, and never knew whether to be suspicious or pleased. "Thanks for your concern, Mr Houseman," she said. "I'll remember your advice."

It worked. He looked away from her, rubbing his knees with knobbly hands. Perspiration glistened on his forehead. Annabel finished the balloon and tied the end while he framed his next sentence.

"Er ... Alan thinks it could be the best thing for you. Him going away, like."

She didn't see how it possibly could be, but she stuck to Lucy's strategy. "I'll remember that, Mr Houseman."

The muscles round his mouth slipped a little. He gave a decisive nod, as if to bring the conversation to an end. "Well, anyway. It's nice to have a little talent, isn't it?"

Annabel put the balloon pump down so hastily it fell off the wall on the field side and lay among the buttercups. "It certainly is, Mr Houseman."

"Here, lass, let me do that," he said, putting down his beer. He picked up the pump, fitted a balloon onto the nozzle and began to pump

30

very fast. "How many does she want done?"

Annabel shrugged. Truly, she didn't care. She got up from the wall. "I'd better go in now. Thanks for doing that, Mr Houseman."

"Frank," he said, without conviction. "And see you keep on with the art, won't you?"

Annabel frowned, and looked at him. "I don't think I will," she said. "I'm too boring to do anything."

Why was she telling him? It wasn't his business. She didn't even want him to know. But here she was, telling him.

He stopped blowing up the balloon. He was embarrassed. "Annabel..."

His small black eyes looked straight at her for a moment. "Look – don't worry, lass. Everything'll work out, as sure as horse manure is good for roses."

It was one of Dad's expressions. Annabel's heart did something funny. "And bad for noses," she added, like Dad always had.

Frank Houseman didn't smile, but the muscles in his neck relaxed. "That's right. Now, you get off upstairs and change out of them jeans. I like to see a pretty little girl like you in a frock."

Back to square one, thought Annabel as she climbed the stairs.

NOT A TOURIST

The morning after the party Annabel awoke in a broad stripe of sunlight. She rolled over and stretched. The pink bunny on the alarm clock Dad had brought back years ago from Blackpool told her with his paws that it was a quarter to eleven.

The house was silent. Janet was still asleep, and would be for hours. Annabel went to the bathroom and washed sketchily, trying not to make a noise. She slipped on dirty jeans and an old cotton blouse which had shrunk and showed her midriff. She left her hair unbrushed and her nose shining, because there was no one to see her. Except Norman, who wouldn't mind.

Downstairs there was a strong smell of cigarette smoke. She opened the door to the garden as wide as it would go and picked up Norman. He mewed, showing the pink inside

32

of his mouth.

"Are you hungry? Are you thirsty?" she asked, cuddling him with more enthusiasm than he liked. "All right, then, your Norman-ness, your servant will obey."

The storm hadn't come. Outside the kitchen door the sun lit the garden so brightly that it sparkled. The air was absolutely, perfectly still. Annabel listened to the bees droning in the honeysuckle, and the rustle of a thrush's feathers in the lilac bush. She almost felt that she could hear the ants scurrying up and down the path.

Norman mewed again. "Here you are, you old lunatic," she said, putting the bowl of food down. "I hope it tastes less disgusting than it smells."

She turned on the tap and let the water run until it was very cold. Plain water was good for the complexion, she'd read in a magazine. She filled a glass and sipped, not liking it much. Then, with impatience, she tipped the rest down the sink.

A day like this demanded a walk. All her life Annabel had taken her problems on rambles and lost them on the way. And today – so still, so chocolate-box perfect – stood ready to receive any anger or misery she cared to inflict on it. Closing the kitchen door as softly as the rusted latch would allow, she set off across the field at the back of the cottage.

This way it was possible to avoid the village altogether, and keep to the country until the main road to Horwell curved round to meet the public path. About half a mile along the Horwell road you could duck under a stone arch and find yourself in a tunnel paved by boulders strewn across a shallow stream, and roofed by silver birches.

Annabel was very fond of the silver tunnel, as she and Lucy used to call the path years ago. They had secretly shared the idea of the tunnel being the one in *The Twelve Dancing Princesses*.

She didn't feel angry or miserable. Perhaps it was something to do with being in the peace of the silver tunnel, but she felt a sense of emptiness. What did it matter that the only person at home who knew how to treat her was Norman? What did it matter that she and Dad would never again toast crumpets at the gas fire in his front room while he listened to the football results? That was what kids did with their dads, and she wasn't a kid any more.

Someone was coming along the path the other way. This was so unusual that Annabel gasped aloud, looking round for somewhere to hide. Today of all days, when she would much rather have been left alone, she couldn't face the prospect of some cheerful intruder.

Making for the trees, she scrambled up the bank at the side of the path. But her feet dislodged some small stones and sent them tumbling into the stream. She heard the panting and put-putting footsteps of a dog.

It was a young spaniel. Its nose was near the ground and the tips of its ears were matted with mud. Annabel liked dogs. She watched this one affectionately as it sniffed her ankles.

"Hey, Jed!"

Between the trees Annabel glimpsed a red and white baseball cap. She retreated further up the bank and caught hold of the trunk of a tree. But the dog came with her, trying to lick her hand. "Go away," she hissed. "Go on, go back."

"Jed! Good boy! Here, boy!"

Annabel didn't recognize the dog. And the boy ambling in an oiled, loose-limbed way along the border of the stream was definitely a stranger.

He saw the dog and lunged at its collar. Then, to his embarrassment, he saw Annabel.

The pink shadow thrown across his face by the baseball cap turned one, or even two, shades deeper. He straightened up, digging his feet into the loose stones just like she had done, and wiped his upper lip with the back of his hand. He didn't actually gasp, but looked as astonished to see her as she was to see him.

Jed ran into the stream and splashed between the stones, his tail sending up a silver spray. The boy turned, searching for his balance on the shifting bank. "Jed! Come here!"

Annabel's surprise increased. The boy, who looked about sixteen or a bit older, was not only a stranger but an *American*.

She stood there, one hand resting on the cool birch bark and the other pushing her hair out of her eyes, feeling extremely pleased that Lucy wasn't there. Lucy's bright cheekiness, though helpful in attracting boys in the first place, often obliterated Annabel's chances of speaking to them. But this boy didn't know that. He didn't know that Annabel had never had a proper boyfriend, and that she and algebra had no chance of ever seeing eye to eye. Her reputation for incompetence was hidden from him as securely as the colour of her underwear.

Watching him, she drew in her breath and did the boldest thing she'd ever done.

"Hello," she said. "You're American, aren't you?"

He was about three metres away from her now, on the edge of the stream. He threw a stick for Jed without turning round. Her words had come out so quietly she wondered if he'd heard her, but she knew that saying them again would make her feel a fool.

"Sort of." His voice, too, was a mutter.

She breathed again, and left the trees. As she stood beside him on level ground he seemed long legged, but not unusually tall. When he

36

bent down to take the stick from the spaniel's mouth she tried to absorb what he looked like. Dark hair, pleasant face, white T-shirt, black jeans was all she could manage.

"Are you here on holiday?" she asked.

He straightened up without looking at her. "Sort of," he said again.

"Not many people know this path," she said. "I used to come here and play when I was a little girl."

"You don't say."

She couldn't tell whether this was rude. It was like when Americans on TV said something like "that's too bad", which held sympathy in their language but hostility in hers.

She persevered. "Broughton's a boring place to live in, but tourists always say what a pretty village it is."

The boy hurled the stick far into the trees on the opposite bank. "I'm not a tourist," he said, more clearly. "My father lives right here in Broughton."

"Oh!" Annabel wasn't prepared for this. "Really?"

"Yes, *really*." Jed panted out of the trees and dropped the stick at the boy's feet, then began to run round in hysterical circles. "My dad told me to walk Jed here. It's his regular place."

Annabel pointed through the trees towards Cairncross Farm. "You can walk on this path, but those fields are private. They belong to the farm over there."

For the first time the boy looked squarely at her. His dark eyes were set wide apart, like a young child's. Annabel was aware that what they were seeing was a short girl in filthy jeans, with a midriff unaccustomed to exposure, unwashed hair and a shiny, perspiring face.

"That farm," he said, nodding in the direction she'd pointed. "D'you know the man who lives there?"

"Well, yes. He was at school with my father."

"What's he like?"

Annabel was surprised at his interest in Frank Houseman. "He's OK, I suppose. My mother bought our cottage from him."

The boy took a breath. "Did your mother give a party last night?"

"How do you know that?" asked Annabel in astonishment.

He seemed embarrassed. "Look – the truth is … he's my father."

Annabel's insides jumped. "Oh!" she exclaimed. Then, because her brain was so stunned by this news that it wouldn't work properly, she said something stupid. "But he can't be. He hasn't got a wife or any children."

The boy adjusted the peak of his cap, smiling humourlessly. "Are you kidding? Look, my mother came from America. He sent me there when I was a baby, because she died."

"Oh!" said Annabel again. She didn't know what she had expected the boy's explanation to be, but it certainly wasn't this. Dad didn't talk about Frank Houseman. And Janet, who knew him well, had certainly never mentioned his wife or son. "I – I'm sorry she died."

"So am I." He took off his cap, ruffled his hair and put it back on again. He watched her for a moment from under the red peak. Then he looked towards the farm. "Pretty weird old place, isn't it?"

"I've never been there," she confessed.

"You're not missing much. There's a well in the stable yard, and part of the roof has fallen in. It's prehistoric."

Annabel wanted to say "Oh!" again, but stopped herself.

"I mean, I expected buildings in England to be old, but not buildings that people *live* in." He kicked moodily at a stone. "What does my dad expect me to do for the whole summer, stuck in this place? I've been here since yesterday, and OK, I had jet-lag, and needed to sleep. But why get me over here at all, if he's just going to ignore me?"

Annabel pictured Frank Houseman as she usually saw him, plodding purposefully along the High Street with a newspaper under his arm. "Maybe he'll take some time off when he can, and show you round the local sights," she suggested.

The boy's face took on a contemptuous look. "Can't wait!"

"Americans usually like Yorkshire." Annabel presumed this was true, on the basis of the busloads which descended every summer on York. "It's full of old buildings, as you say. All the tourists go to York Minster. And Haworth, of course, where some famous writers lived."

"So I'm a tourist now, am I?" He stopped kicking the stone. His clear gaze landed on her face again. "What's your name?"

"Annabel."

"*Annabel?*" He narrowed his eyes. "How old are you?"

"Sixteen." Well, fifteen and a half.

His gaze wandered down to her dirty trainers then hurried back up, coming to rest on the sweaty, separating strands of her fringe. "You look more like fourteen."

"I'm not!"

"I bet you're no more than thirteen," said the boy. Then he added, defensively, "I'm seventeen. And my name's Sebastian."

"I know a dog called Sebastian," said Annabel.

She hadn't meant this rudely, but he was very offended. He lowered his shoulders and raised his chin. "Sebastian is a Spanish name. It's the name of a saint. My mother had Mexican ancestry, and I'm very proud of it."

There was a silence. "I'm sorry," said Annabel. "But my aunt, the one with the dog, just happens to call it Sebastian. It's a collie."

"Which way do I go for a store which sells newspapers?" he asked impatiently. "My dad told me to get something called *The Daily Telegram*."

There was still offence in his voice. Annabel knew it was *The Daily Telegraph,* but dared not correct him. She pointed down the stream the way she had come. "If you follow the path it brings you to the road to Broughton. There are shops there, and a pub called the Rose and Crown. Your father's yard is about halfway along the High Street, through an archway."

"Thanks."

He took a dog leash from his pocket and began to fiddle with Jed's collar. Without saying goodbye he yanked the dog to heel and set off in the dappled sunshine towards the village. Annabel watched him for a little while. Then she stuck her hands in her pockets and took off in the opposite direction.

She walked fast, though the sun was directly overhead and she could feel sweat-beads on her temples. List your thoughts mentally, her English teacher Mrs Phillips always said, before you begin your essay. Make notes in pencil if necessary.

Thought One. Sebastian Houseman was a boy just like the one she'd kept inside her head all this time – only much more exotic. He came from America, where people had ranches and pools and stretch limousines. And he certainly looked all right. Even Lucy, whose standards were very high, would have to agree. His occupation of the Boy-free Zone for the entire summer had to be good news. But even better was the fact that *she,* not Lucy, had spoken to him first. It was *she* who had stood her ground and said his name was a dog's name. Which it was.

Thought Two made her heart feel stretched, like a beach ball pumped too full of air. She slowed her pace. Sebastian's father was a well-known Broughton figure, and an old friend of both her parents. Once the village had got over his sudden appearance, Sebastian would be planted in the local landscape as firmly as his father. She was certain to meet him again.

Thought Three was so incredible she would never have risked noting it down, even in pencil. Everyone knew that Annabel Bairstow was the prettiest girl in Broughton. Not very tall, not very extraordinary in any way, but *pretty*, in the truest sense of the word. She knew that her heart-shaped face and small features made her look babyish. But those painted blue eyes with their deep, changing light soon made it clear she wasn't the child people sometimes took her for. Sebastian, whose face had actually gone pink when he saw her, must have noticed. He just *must* have.

The trees thinned and the old sign saying CAIRNCROSS FARM – PLEASE SHUT THE GATE came into sight. Annabel linked her fingers on the weathered gatepost, rested her chin on them and looked at the house with new eyes.

It stood square against the midday sky, as cold and unapproachable as its owner. She dug her knuckles into her chin, wondering why Frank Houseman had let the roof fall in, when he obviously had enough money to get it mended. She wondered which of the windows was Sebastian's room, and pictured him sitting in the stone-walled gloom, wearing his baseball cap and scowling. What would he find to occupy himself between now and the date on his plane ticket?

She turned down the lane which led from Cairncross to the Horwell road.

The shade of the drystone wall beside the lane was narrowing as the sun climbed. Annabel stopped and leaned against the warm grey stones, noticing they weren't grey at all, but a mixture of a thousand colours, with moss growing in crevices here and there. Her shoulder fitted neatly into a hollow between the stones. For a moment, as she stood there thinking and imagining, she felt as if she belonged to the wall, and it to her. She felt as if she could climb inside it, and live there for ever.

Lucy would say she was a sentimental idiot, she knew. But as she set off again in the sliver of shade, she thought how strange it was that however much she loved Broughton, it couldn't love her in return. If you gave love, people said, you would receive it. But how could Annabel receive love, when the person she'd always loved best had gone away, and the only thing left wasn't a person at all, but a place?

ULTERIOR MOTIVE

"An *American*? A tourist, you mean?"

Lucy, who was halfway through a Brown's Banana Buster, propped up her spoon, her eyes stretching. "I'm not going to eat another mouthful until you tell me all about him!"

Annabel laughed. The more she thought about Sebastian, the more clearly she saw how nice he'd looked. His white T-shirt had suited him. His arms weren't bony like Sean Turnbull's, and his shoulders didn't slope so much. Even Lucy's failure to turn up and help with the party mess hadn't squashed her conviction that life was about to get better.

Lucy's spoon slumped against the side of her glass. "Come *on*, Barb," she pleaded.

"Don't call me that. And get on with your ice-cream before it turns into a drink."

"Stop being so bossy." Lucy took up her spoon again. "Honestly, Annabel, anyone would think you'd never met a boy before."

"Well, I haven't."

Every Saturday since they'd first been allowed to go to Horwell alone Annabel and Lucy had spent the evening at the window table of Brown's American Bar. It wasn't really a bar at all but a café and ice-cream parlour, and it wasn't very American either. The best thing about the place, apart from its tolerance of teenagers with a lot of time and very little money, was the ice-cream. And the best thing about the ice-cream was the recent appointment of a cheerful boy in a paper hat and white jacket to serve it. As he turned to flip some coins into the till he clicked his heels and pushed his chest out, like the Von Trapp children in *The Sound of Music*, grinning toothily at Annabel.

"You see?" said Annabel, lowering her voice. "*That's* the sort of boy I usually meet."

Lucy's eyebrows twitched. "But he's sweet!"

"He's got freckles, Luce."

"So?"

Annabel was suddenly tired of messing about. She pushed her own ice-cream dish aside and folded her arms on the table. "The boy's name's Sebastian. He's seventeen, and he's got dark hair and a nice smiley face, and he's not too tall, and—"

"But what's he doing here, in Broughton?"

"Oh, Lucy, that's the best part!" Annabel unfolded her arms and clasped her hands. It felt like that moment on Christmas Day, when the largest, most expensive-looking present was about to surrender its secret. "He's visiting his father for the whole summer. And can you imagine who his father is?"

"Of course not, you moron."

"Frank Houseman!"

Lucy said nothing. Her mouth was forming a silent circle.

"I know it's strange, that he's never been to England before." Annabel began to fiddle energetically with a paper serviette. "I mean, I never knew Frank Houseman even *had* a son. Did you?"

Lucy wasn't pleased, or excited, or any of the things Annabel had thought she'd be. Her golden skin actually paled before Annabel's eyes, making Annabel acutely conscious of her own rising colour. In Lucy's eyes there was an expression which Annabel couldn't understand.

She put down the serviette. "What's the matter, Luce?"

Lucy looked at her for a long moment. "I think I *did* know, actually. I remember being in the newspaper shop, and Mrs Evans was talking to my mum about Frank Houseman's wife dying in an accident. She thought it was scandalous that he sent his son away. I don't think she likes him much. Mind you, Mrs Evans gossips about everyone, so—"

"When was this? *When*?" asked Annabel, feeling that she had been excluded from something important.

Lucy licked the sweet ice-cream residue off her spoon. "Last summer? The summer before?"

Annabel didn't feel happy, or in control, or anything she'd felt before. "Why didn't you mention it to me?"

"I didn't even remember it, until now." She frowned at Annabel. "And anyway, you must know more about Frank Houseman than I do. Your dad went to school with him, didn't he? And he and Janet seem to see a lot of each other these days."

Annabel felt a fool. What if everyone in Broughton knew about Sebastian, except her? Even those who, like Lucy, weren't even born when his mother had died?

"He only comes round to fix things for Janet," she said defensively. "He used to own the cottage, you know. He's the only one who can make the boiler work."

Lucy was looking at her with sympathy. "Have you told Janet you've met Sebastian?"

Annabel sighed. "I haven't spoken to her. She didn't surface until three o'clock, and she only came out of her room for some aspirins."

"She must know he's here, though,"

reasoned Lucy.

"Oh, yes! I suppose so. It's odd though – neither she nor Frank said anything about him last night."

Lucy raised her eyebrows. "Last night?"

"At the party."

"Frank Houseman was at the party?"

"Yes."

"Oh!" Lucy considered. "Well, I suppose he would be."

"Honestly, Luce, it was gruesome. Janet had on that hideous blue shiny outfit, and she insisted on *dancing*. Well, trying to."

"How gross."

There was a silence. Annabel scratched the bottom of her ice-cream dish with her spoon. "Perhaps she wants Sebastian to be a surprise for me," she suggested. "That would be typical. But—"

Suddenly, a picture as bright as a Kodachrome advertisement came into her mind. It was of Sebastian kicking a stone and saying, "But why get me over here at all, if he's just going to ignore me?" Maybe Janet wasn't the only parent whose good intentions didn't always work out.

"But what?" asked Lucy.

"Sometimes I don't want surprises. I'd prefer her just to tell me things."

Lucy grasped the edge of the table and pushed her chair forwards with her bottom.

Annabel watched her, remembering a childish fantasy that Lucy wasn't the daughter of Mr and Mrs Alderson at all, but a gypsy changeling. She felt pleased that the real Lucy Alderson had been left to take her chance with the gypsies.

When Lucy spoke, Annabel detected an unexpected coldness – a kind of withered quality – in her voice.

"Don't take this the wrong way, Annabel," she said carefully. "But don't be surprised if Sebastian's visit turns out to have ... oh, you know, an ulterior motive."

Annabel gazed at her with wide eyes, not understanding.

"You look like a fish," said Lucy.

"What do you mean, an ulterior motive?"

An anxious look came over Lucy's face. She tugged at one of her curls, winding it tightly round her finger and releasing it, and winding it again. "Well..." She paused, and made a decision. "Look, Barb, forget it. Just forget I said it."

Annabel studied the metal strip around the edge of the table, feeling unsettled. It was bad enough that Janet treated her like a child who shouldn't ask awkward questions, without Lucy doing it too. Why couldn't she just say what she meant?

Lucy pushed back her chair. "I'll get some coffee, shall I?"

Annabel hated Brown's coffee, which came in a cup too shallow to pick up without tilting it. "I'd rather have an Apple Fizz," she said, reaching for her bag.

"Put your purse away, silly."

While Lucy was at the counter the glass swing-door opened and a boy in a baseball cap came in. Annabel's stomach contracted. It was Sebastian.

NICE BOY

As Sebastian approached the counter Annabel recognized his gangly walk. He was still wearing the black jeans, with a light zip-up jacket over his T-shirt. He looked fit, she noticed, but not heavy. Perhaps he was good at some sport, like most boys considered themselves to be. Football, probably, if they had football in America.

Lucy had noticed him too. Watching their backs, Annabel felt her digestive system disintegrate further, until it resembled something powdery. Sawdust, perhaps. Her mouth seemed to be full of the same stuff.

Sebastian was searching the pockets of his jacket for some money. Annabel saw his face in three-quarter view as he glanced at Lucy. When Lucy's order came she put some of her change in her pocket but dropped the rest of the coins on the floor. How could she be so *obvious*? Sebastian stamped on them and helped her pick them up, and Lucy smiled prettily at him. Leaning on the counter like a gunslinger, he watched her walk self-consciously back to the table.

"Did you see *that*?" Lucy's voice was a breathless whisper. "Did you see me pretend to drop my change? What a—"

There was no point in postponing the inevitable. Annabel sighed. "Lucy – that's Sebastian."

Lucy's face seemed to inflate, as her eyes expanded and her jaw dropped. Annabel wondered if she should tell *her* she looked like a fish. "Why didn't you tell me what he looks like?"

"I *did*."

"But you didn't tell me he was so drop-dead dishy!"

Annabel was so astonished that she almost forgot to whisper. "Lucy, for heaven's sake! That's the sort of thing Laura Turnbull would say."

"Well, I think he's—"

"Lucy!"

Sebastian had collected a can of Coke and was standing beside their table.

"So this is where you hang out, is it, Anne-Marie?" he said to Annabel.

Annabel knew that the colour which had begun on her neck was rising higher and higher, covering her whole face. Even her ears. "Yes, I suppose so. And my name's—"

"Who's this?" he asked, waving the can at Lucy. "Your sister?"

Lucy had located and dragged from its hiding-place every scrap of flirtatious behaviour she knew. She pushed a chair out with her foot, smiling up at Sebastian. Her eyes shone as she watched him sit down. The curl which she'd been twisting round her finger lay in a cluster of others against her smooth, pink-gold cheek. She slid her hand beneath them and lifted them away, exposing one small ear with its glittering earring, then let her hair fall back over it with a tiny shake of her head. "No, I'm her mother," she quipped.

Concentrate, Annabel told herself. Ignore her. It was *you* who struck gold in the silver tunnel. You've got to stake your claim.

Sebastian grinned, his upper teeth coming over his lower lip. He opened the can, sipped from it, put it down and wiped his mouth with the back of his hand. Then he took off his jacket, hooking it over the back of his chair. "Is she always this cute, Anne-Marie?"

"*Annabel*," said Annabel. "And this is Lucy."

Lucy blinked at him. "You're Frank Houseman's son, aren't you?"

"That's right," said Sebastian, dangling his

arm over the back of the chair. "Do you know him?"

"Yes. Well, no. I mean, everyone in Broughton knows him, really. Annabel and I are at the same school. Did she tell you that?"

Lucy had started doing what she always did. Getting in front of Annabel's attempts to talk to boys. Annabel noticed she didn't say that they'd been inseparable friends for ten years. Perhaps that sounded too little-girl.

Sebastian sat forward. "Not in the same class, surely? You must be at least sixteen."

Lucy flushed with pleasure.

"She's fifteen," said Annabel ungraciously. "We both are."

She picked up her straw and stabbed the ice cubes which floated on top of the Apple Fizz, waiting for him to reveal her childish lie. But he said nothing.

The waitress brought his burger. "Ketchup?" she asked.

Sebastian lifted the top half of the bun gingerly. "Sure," he said. "And some relish. And where's the salad?"

The waitress shrugged, put the ketchup bottle on the table and walked away.

Sebastian put ketchup on the burger and bit into it. Even without relish or salad, he seemed to enjoy it. "What kind of a burger place is this anyway?" he said through the next bite. "The sign outside says AMERICAN BAR. They must be

55

kidding!"

"You're lucky to get ketchup," Lucy told him. "This isn't New York – it's Old York!"

Sebastian smiled so broadly that some half-chewed burger almost fell out of his mouth.

"If you want a proper burger you'll have to go to York or Harrogate. Or somewhere bigger than Horwell, anyway," explained Annabel.

"Somewhere that isn't such a hole, you mean?"

Annabel and Lucy exchanged a look. Then Lucy took charge.

"Annabel says you're over here for the whole summer," she said. "That should give you plenty of time to get to know your father."

"Yeah," said Sebastian, licking ketchup off his fingertips.

"It must be strange, meeting him again after so long."

"Yeah."

"I mean, how did he recognize you at the airport?"

Sebastian stopped eating. "Oh, he's been over to see me a couple of times. Well, once. And my aunt sends him photos and stuff."

Annabel looked at his sunburned skin and the casual expensiveness of the jacket hanging on the back of his chair. Frank Houseman would bring him to the cottage soon, she was certain. Janet would offer him a chocolate

56

biscuit and ask him why ninety-two per cent of men *still* never did the ironing, which was what she always did with male visitors. She wouldn't notice that he was a creature from a different world, who had landed on a planet with an atmosphere unable to sustain his particular form of life.

Apprehension began to creep up on her. "Er … did you find the newspaper shop?" she asked him while Lucy was sipping coffee.

"Sure." He waited for the next question, like a movie star being interviewed for a magazine.

"Of course he did!" said Lucy in her I'm-in-charge way. "You'd have to be a complete deadhead to get lost in a place the size of Broughton!"

Annabel ignored her. "Which part of America do you live in?"

"California."

"Los Angeles?" Lucy looked excited. "Hollywood?"

"Not exactly," said Sebastian. "Outside Los Angeles. In the suburbs."

"In Beverly Hills?" prompted Lucy.

"No, not in Beverly Hills. Though my aunt goes shopping there sometimes."

Annabel wondered what shopping in Beverly Hills would be like. For clothes which cost hundreds of dollars, she supposed. Or jewellery which cost thousands. Sebastian's aunt and uncle must be very wealthy. No wonder he considered Cairncross prehistoric and Horwell a hole. Perhaps, she admitted unwillingly to herself, the little corner of Yorkshire she knew and loved so well was less desirable than she'd realized.

Sebastian took another bite of his burger and chewed it. "Either of you girls ever been to the States?" he asked.

They shook their heads. "I've been to Marbella," volunteered Lucy.

"Yeah?" said Sebastian, mystified.

Annabel sipped her Apple Fizz, taking care not to make a slurping noise. She looked at Lucy, who was looking at Sebastian, who was mopping up ketchup with his burger bun. She knew that she and Lucy were in a race to start the next part of the conversation, but she couldn't think of anything to say which Sebastian might want to hear. Lucy always won those races, anyway.

"How did you get to Horwell? By bus?"

Lucy's question seemed to surprise him. He waited a moment before he answered, looking from one to the other of the girls. "By *bus*? Are you kidding? No, I hitched a ride on a truck. I don't travel on buses."

Lucy slid her elbows forward on the table. "You've got your own car, then? In America, I mean."

He gave her a tolerant smile.

"Is it a convertible?" she asked. "Like they have on TV, when they climb over the doors?"

"Yeah." He was proud of it, Annabel could hear. "It was a birthday present from my uncle and aunt."

They must be *really* wealthy, thought Annabel. "What's your uncle's job?" she asked before Lucy could speak.

Sebastian's mouth was full of burger again. "He's a –" He swallowed the mouthful. "He's a psychiatrist. And my aunt works in a library. What do your folks do?"

What Janet did sounded much more impressive than working in a library. For once, Annabel announced it without embarrassment. "My mother's a student at the University of York. She takes her degree next year."

"Is that so?"

"Yes. She—"

"My Aunt Martha has a PhD in Library Science." Sebastian brushed some crumbs off his T-shirt, not looking at either of the girls. "She works at UCLA."

Lucy giggled. "At *what*?"

"University of California, Los Angeles," he explained calmly. He pushed his plate away and began to drum his fingers on the top of his Coke can, clicking his nails. "I'm going there in the fall."

Annabel's heart sank. Sebastian was not only good-looking, well-dressed and the owner of a car. He was brainy, too. What must he think of these witless English girls, two years too young for a driving licence and one year short of any possible qualifications?

There was a pause, and then it happened.

It was an accident. The can Sebastian was fiddling with skidded across the table. As he tried to stop it his wrist landed firmly on the fleshy part of Annabel's forearm, just below the crook of her elbow. Not his hand exactly, just his wrist, and he withdrew it so quickly Annabel wasn't even sure that Lucy noticed.

But when she looked at the place on her arm, she felt again the warmth and slight stickiness, and the indescribable, unexpected *boyness* of his skin. Her own skin began to tingle. Her breath disappeared. It wasn't the same as touching Lucy or Dad or Janet, or the boys who had kissed her clumsily in the cinema or danced with her at discos in the Horwell Scout Hut. It wasn't the same as touching anybody she'd ever touched before.

Once, in an art lesson, Mr Lefevre had asked her class to look at some pictures with their eyes screwed up. Someone had asked him why this made them appear clearer, and he had explained that eyes automatically sharpen their focus for a moment if you narrow them, and that's why artists "squint" at what they're drawing.

Annabel was reminded of Mr Lefevre's

60

words as she sat there in Brown's with the world re-focusing more clearly around her. She felt like Alice at the bottom of the rabbit hole, when she finally squeezed through that tiny door to the beautiful garden.

She looked at the reflection of Sebastian's profile in the window. Without the roundness of his face to disguise them his nose and forehead looked bony, like Frank Houseman's. A light from the street shone on his cap, outlining it with an orangey glow. He was smiling at something Lucy was saying, his lips drawn back from glittering teeth which Annabel supposed had been straightened and polished by an American orthodontist. He looked foreign, for sure. But he looked nice, too.

Her heart skidded, and her imagination took flight. Maybe Sebastian was the nice boy she'd been waiting for all this time. She wasn't dreaming him, and she certainly hadn't dreamed his touch. Maybe – she had to control her breathing as she thought about this – maybe, when he'd touched her arm, he'd felt something too.

What did a girl's skin feel like to a boy?

Maybe, when school started again and he had to go back to America, he would take with him more than the memory of an idle summer spent in a Yorkshire valley. Maybe for once in her life something would go right, and her blue eyes would smile at him from the picture he would carry in his wallet.

Maybe he'd take it out and look at it on the plane, and smile back at it.

And maybe, even when he'd put the picture back in its hiding place, he'd remember her, and smile again.

PART TWO

The Stone Horse

DREAMBOAT

Annabel lay on a towel under the copper beech in the cottage garden. She was reading a book called *The Dreamboat of Firewater Lake*, which Laura Turnbull had lent to Lucy and Lucy had lent to her. "Fifty-nine to sixty-one," Lucy had whispered as she'd stuffed the book into Annabel's bag. "*Hot*. I can say no more."

Hot indeed. The hero and heroine were stranded on an island in the middle of a lake – Annabel had skipped the bit which explained how they'd got there – and were splashing in the shallows. There was a long description of the sunset's fiery rage, then the heroine found herself pinned to the beach by the hero's muscular but tender embrace.

"Annabel! Do you want a doughnut?" called Janet from the kitchen window.

"No, thank you!" Annabel slid the book under the towel.

Janet came out of the house wearing a sun hat. She sat down heavily in a deck-chair, selected a doughnut and bit into it. "Frank's coming over later, darling. I've invited him to Sunday lunch. Won't that be nice?" She rescued a globule of jam from the corner of her mouth. "He's got his son visiting from America, so he's bringing him too."

Annabel couldn't resist demolishing Janet's news, as Lucy had demolished hers. She reached for her bottle of sun block. "Sebastian, do you mean?"

"Oh – so you *do* know about him!" She swallowed her mouthful. "I thought you did, but Frank ... well, never mind. Anyway, you'd like to meet him, I'm sure."

"I've met him already."

Janet stared. "Really, Annabel, you do talk nonsense sometimes! How can you have met him? He only arrived on Friday, and Frank says he spent most of yesterday asleep."

Annabel smeared sun block on her knee with more care than it needed. Her heart felt restless. "Well, he wasn't asleep when I met him up by Cairncross. He was taking Frank's dog for a walk. And he came into Brown's last night when Lucy and I were there."

"*Well!*" said Janet after a short, stiff silence.

"I'm sorry, Janet. I didn't plan it." That rhymes, she thought, and smiled.

"Well, I planned it!" Janet didn't look

amused. "And you can stop smirking, young lady. What about *my* plans? You never think, do you? You never bother to consider for one second that *I* exist too, do you?"

Annabel tipped the bottle and began on the other leg. "But how was I to know who Sebastian was? And I've never even seen Frank Houseman's dog before. He must walk him at midnight, or something. And anyway, everyone in Broughton seems to have forgotten Sebastian exists, if they ever knew. Even you and Dad don't talk about him."

Janet, who couldn't deny this, wouldn't look at her. She shrugged her shoulders. The front of her loose cotton dress shuddered.

"Oh, come on," persevered Annabel. "What have you arranged for today?"

Janet's disappointment hadn't diminished her appetite. She took another bite of the doughnut, and chewed and swallowed before she spoke. "I hoped Frank would bring Sebastian to the party on Friday. That's why I wanted you to be there – so you could get to know each other. But apparently the boy refused to come, saying he was jet-lagged." She glanced moodily at Annabel. "And if I'd known you two were such bosom pals already, I wouldn't have bothered to ask them to lunch."

"I've only seen him twice, Janet."

"Well, that's twice more than I have." Janet

67

tilted the brim of her hat and looked at the trees on the other side of the field. "Anyway, Frank says he's a moody little monster. And cheeky, too. He asked to borrow the car, for heaven's sake!" She gave Annabel a testing, sideways look. "So Frank's decided he's got to find things for him to do. Would the Turnbulls sign him in at the tennis club, do you think?"

Annabel's stomach did a back-flip. "Today, you mean?"

"Yes, this afternoon. Apparently Sebastian's desperate to play tennis, and the Turnbull boy's pretty good, isn't he? He'll give him a match. Why don't you get him and Lucy, and the Turnbull girl – what's her name?"

"Laura."

"Laura, to come over for lunch too? Frank wants Sebastian to meet people of his own age." She licked sugar off her thumb. "Go on. Why not?"

Sean Turnbull *and* Sebastian? "Janet, I can't."

Janet's look sharpened, then became a knowing one. "Oh, I see how it is. You've got a little crush, haven't you?"

Hot-cheeked, Annabel put on her sun-glasses. "Don't be so *stupid*, Janet."

"Well! I've suspected for ages there's some-thing going on with that Turnbull boy – what's his name?"

Relief almost made Annabel smile, but not

quite. "Sean."

"Oh, of course it is. So, has he asked you out?"

"No. And I'm not interested, anyway."

"Rubbish," said Janet, sitting back in her deck-chair, her gold mules only just touching the grass. Her mood had thawed a little. The dreamy look which she had when she was watching a romantic film on TV came into her eyes. "He's just the right age for you, you know. And his people are very pleasant. His mother told me he's applying to Oxford next term."

Listen to the liberated woman, thought Annabel. Janet was always sticking stickers on the fridge which said things like "Sisterhood, Motherhood, Misunderstood", or "Men may be Maggots, but Women are not Worms", but she never applied feminist theory to real people's lives. Especially Annabel's.

"Are you going to phone, then?"

Still Annabel hesitated. Dread and excitement sparred jerkily in her chest. Sean Turnbull had never been to the cottage before, because she'd never had an excuse to invite him. Until now, when she would rather not invite him at all.

"Go *on*," urged Janet. "My roast chicken will be as dry as a ball of string if you don't hurry up." She gasped, remembering something. "Goodness! I hope there's enough food.

How many did I say?"

"Seven, including us. Though Laura Turnbull will eat enough for at least two."

Janet calculated. "Oh, that's all right. If there isn't enough you can pretend you're not hungry. Go and phone now. And tell them not to forget their kit. Sebastian's bringing his."

The thought of Sebastian in his tennis kit made Annabel's insides feel scrambled. But her next thought – that she'd never learned either the rules or the technique of tennis – unscrambled them again. Of course, she wouldn't have to *play*. She would leave it to Laura and Lucy to get red-faced and sweaty while she watched from the clubhouse in dark glasses, like a film star at Wimbledon.

She stood up, leaving *The Dreamboat of Firewater Lake* in its hiding place.

"I wonder what Sebastian thought of Lucy Alderson," mused Janet, the last piece of doughnut suspended between her fingers, two centimetres from her lips. "She gave him the treatment, I suppose?"

Annabel was halfway across the lawn. She looked back at her mother. "What's that supposed to mean?"

Janet gave her one of her frozen-yogurt looks. Sweet, but cold, and slightly sour. "That child would flirt with her own left ear, if she could see it."

"Janet, she's not a *child*. And she didn't put

70

her hand on his knee under the table, if that's what you're thinking. It's *your* friends who do that sort of thing."

She turned to go into the house.

"Try not to be annoying, won't you, darling girl?" called Janet. "Let's make an effort to give them a nice day."

ROMANTIC FRICTION

But Frank and Sebastian didn't seem to be having a nice day at all. It was obvious to Annabel as soon as they arrived at the cottage that they'd been arguing.

"So this is Sebastian!" Janet click-clicked down the garden path, beaming rosily, with both hands outstretched. "Goodness, Frank, he's nearly as tall as you!"

Sebastian stepped backwards so hastily that his foot landed in Janet's geranium bed. Annabel put her hand over her mouth. But Janet laughed.

"Oh, never mind about that. Come and sit down, and tell me all about yourself. You've already met Annabel, haven't you?"

Annabel was glad she'd put on her black dress, even though Janet always said it only needed the ruby slippers to complete the costume for the Wicked Witch of the West. Frank and Sebastian were both wearing ironed shirts. Sebastian's baseball cap was white, with a logo on the front. Under it his face looked darker than the shadow it cast.

"Sure," he said sulkily.

"We've got several young people for you to meet today, Sebastian," said Janet. "And I hope you've brought your appetite with you! Now, would you like tea, or lemonade?"

Shut up, Janet, thought Annabel. Just shut *up*. He drinks coffee, not tea. And he doesn't want to be sent off with his little friends to play in the treehouse. Sebastian and his father sat down on the wall. Annabel began to feel very hot. Then she remembered that the towel she was sitting on still concealed *The Dreamboat of Firewater Lake*, and felt hotter still.

Sebastian didn't say anything to Janet. He looked at the ground.

"Frank?" said Janet, bewildered.

Frank jabbed Sebastian's thigh with his forefinger. "Don't you be so damned rude, boy. Janet's invited you to her house, and—"

"And I didn't want to come, if you remember," muttered Sebastian.

"That's *enough*!"

"Is it too hot for you out here, Sebastian?" suggested Janet brightly.

Sebastian's head came up fast. "You call this *hot*? Jeez, you must be kidding!"

"Sebastian, for the last time!" Frank's

73

gloomy face had flushed. "If you can't behave in a civilized way there'll be no tennis this afternoon or any afternoon. Do you understand me?"

A muscle in Sebastian's cheek twitched. His teeth showed, but he didn't quite smile. "It's all right, Mrs – er…" he said to Janet. "I'm fine here. D'you have a beer? A cold one?"

Janet's face fell. "No."

"Get him a coffee, Janet," said Frank impatiently. "Instant will do."

"I hate—" began Sebastian, but was interrupted by another jab, this time in his shoulder. "Hey, that hurts!"

His father was unrepentant. "It was supposed to, smart-arse."

Sebastian was sitting with his elbows on his knees and his chin in his hands. A line of earthenware begonia pots stood to attention on the wall beside him. Around him spread the familiar view of the green and yellow field and the different green of the trees behind it. Surrounded by nature, he looked unnatural, ill at ease.

Frank stood up, muttering about helping Janet in the kitchen. "And you might as well give up trying to be awkward, my lad," he told Sebastian grimly, "because you'll soon discover that I can be damned awkward myself."

Sebastian shrugged, and was silent.

Here was Annabel's second opportunity to

speak to him alone. She knew she shouldn't waste it. She should get up and sit in the place his father had just vacated. She should get him to look into her face, and moisten her lips and blink. She'd seen other girls do those things millions of times, and she'd practised them in front of the bathroom mirror with the door locked. But she stayed sitting on the towel, and the warm midday air hovered between them, full of silence.

Then Sebastian raised his head. Hesitantly, like the flash-dazzle-blink of a fluorescent light, a smile struggled out. "My dad and I had a fight," he said in a rush, like a confession. "He won't let me borrow his car. He thinks I can't drive in England, but I bet I can. I mean, all you have to do is drive on the left, don't you? Easy."

Annabel made an effort to keep the conversation going. "Perhaps he thinks you can't handle such a big car."

"Listen, there's no way that jumped-up rabbit my dad drives is any bigger than Scobie's station wagon, and I drive that all the time."

She had never thought of Frank's mud-splashed Range Rover as a jumped-up rabbit. She didn't know whether she was supposed to laugh. "Is Scobie your uncle?"

"Yeah. His name's Stuart, but no one calls him that." He considered for a moment. "Hey, maybe I can get *him* to persuade my dad I'm a good driver. I'll call him." He looked at his wristwatch, then at Annabel, but he didn't seem to see her. His mind was on something else. "What time is it in California right now?"

"I don't know," she confessed. "I'm sorry."

The peak of Sebastian's cap turned away from her. "After about six o'clock should be OK. They must be quite a few hours behind us, but at least I won't get them out of bed."

Annabel felt defeated. If he already knew, why had he asked her? The excitement she'd felt when he'd started to talk to her turned into a trickle of disappointment. It dripped into her stomach, making her feel sick. He'd suspected she was a dumb kid, and now he knew.

"And meanwhile, I'll keep working on my dad," said Sebastian. He put his chin back into his hands. "He's bound to give in eventually."

A crash came from the house, followed by a female voice swearing. Sebastian looked up. "Does your mom often use words like that?"

The sound of the glass breaking had given Annabel an idea. "What about – to get the car off your dad, I mean – what about incapacitating him?" she suggested.

He took his hands away from his chin. He rolled his eyes and made a mock-outraged face. "Wussat, honey? You tellin' me to break his legs or somethin'?"

When people put on silly voices Annabel

was usually half-envious, half-embarrassed. But Sebastian's silly voice amused her, and she laughed. The muscles in his face moved, but too minutely, and too quickly, for her to read the expression they made.

"Nothing so drastic!" she assured him. "Just keep filling up his wine glass. He'll have to let you drive him home then, unless he wants to get arrested, won't he?"

"Neat idea, Annabel." His face was straight and calm again. "Pity he didn't bring the car."

Lucy crossed the lawn, her legs smooth and golden under a short skirt. "Another baseball cap!" She tweaked the peak of Sebastian's cap playfully. "How many of these have you got? I bet you never play baseball in them!"

Lucy had been followed, more timorously, by Sean and Laura. Conscious that her breath wasn't going in or coming out properly, Annabel got up from the towel. "Sebastian, this is Sean Turnbull, and his sister Laura."

"Hi, Sean," said Sebastian pleasantly. He stood up, holding out his hand. Annabel tried not to notice that his politeness to Sean exaggerated his rudeness to Janet. "Great day for a match."

She watched the boys looking each other up and down. Sebastian was the taller, but his wide eyes gave him a coltish look. Sean, she noticed with surprise, had the more mature face. He gripped Sebastian's hand in a tense,

English sort of way. "Hello," he said.

Laura was staring at Sebastian with round eyes. Annabel wanted to smile. Somewhere there was an unsuspecting boy, devoted as a dog and brainless as a budgie, waiting to be Laura's husband. But for now, she still had her dreams.

"Sean says you're not going to play," said Lucy to Annabel. "Is that right?"

Everyone looked at Annabel, who had sat down again on the towel. "I'm no good at tennis," she admitted. "I'd much rather watch."

"Well, I'm playing," said Laura shyly, looking at no one. "I've brought my dress. So if Annabel plays as well that'll be too many for mixed doubles, anyway."

"You can keep the score, Barb," said Lucy, though she knew Annabel couldn't. "You can call it out like they do on the telly." She put on a posh voice. "New balls, please!"

Sebastian settled himself on the wall, his placid gaze beaming past Lucy's shoulder. Annabel thought at first that he was watching Norman rolling on the grass, but as she turned back she realized he was looking at *her*. "Why does Lucy call you Barb?" he asked curiously. "She did it last night, too. In the States it's short for Barbara, but—"

"Here it's short for Barbie-Brain!" declared Lucy, suppressing Laura's snorts. She glanced

78

gleefully at Annabel. "Isn't it, Annabel?"

Annabel didn't answer. With her forefinger, she traced the outline of a blue and yellow starfish on the towel.

"It's her nickname at school," explained Laura to Sebastian.

Sebastian seemed to choke on something. Coughing, he looked across at Annabel with disbelief and amusement. "Why do they call you that?"

"Well..." Annabel traced another starfish. She'd never been asked to justify the nickname before. Everyone at Hilda Greenaway McDowd accepted it without question. "I suppose people think – though it's only a joke, of course – that I look a bit like a Barbie doll."

There was a pause. Annabel's face began to feel hot. "You know, because of my fair hair and blue eyes."

Sebastian made a strangled sound. "And the 'Brain' bit – what does that mean?"

Annabel swallowed. "I'm – I'm not sure."

All the girls were embarrassed. Lucy twisted round and looked sharply at Laura. "*You* don't call Annabel that, do you?" she demanded.

"No, never," said Laura, her eyebrows raised in alarm.

"And hardly anyone else does, either," said Lucy, twisting back to Sebastian.

"But *you* do," he pointed out. Reasonably,

Annabel thought.

"Oh, no!" protested Lucy. "I mean, I was joking. I just say it sometimes as a sort of habit. It doesn't mean we think Annabel's a dimwit or anything." She was unsure how to go on. She put her hand to her cheek. "God, I'm stupid."

Sean, who had been sitting silently in Janet's deck-chair, entered the conversation. "If you ask me," he said in a no-nonsense voice, "it's the *name* that's stupid. What sort of mean-minded joker thought of it in the first place?"

"Lucy," supplied Laura.

During the silence which followed, Sebastian sat down cross-legged beside Annabel on the towel. He was close enough for her to see the pores where the hairs on his arms came out, and the shadow of his eyelashes against his cheekbone.

"Well, I like it," he said emphatically. "I think it's a great name for an artistic person like Annabel." He looked round the circle of faces. "Hey, didn't you know? She may be little, but Annabel has a big talent. Yes sir, my dad told me she's a *painter*." He said this as if being a painter was OK, but somehow cheesy too. "She sure has some colourful ideas on dealing with parents, I can tell you. Ow!" He'd put his ankle on something hard-edged. "What the hell's this?" He lifted the corner of the towel and found *The Dreamboat of*

Firewater Lake.

Grinning, he read the title aloud. "D'you think we're old enough for this, Sean?"

Annabel made a grab for it, but Sebastian whisked it away with a long arm, far above her head. Sean struggled out of the deck-chair and took it from his hand before Lucy or Laura could reach it. He began to read aloud the first page, which described the heroine's sunkissed hair and silver-grey Pontiac as she drove into the parking lot at Firewater Lake.

"Oh God, it's an American book," groaned Sebastian, standing up and looking over Sean's shoulder. "Hey girls, does it get any steamier than this?"

Laura was pink. "Give me back my book and grow up, will you, Sean?"

Sean made a vacant face at her. "*Your* book?"

Lucy, who was about his height, made a lunge for it, but he threw it to Sebastian, who was taller. "Laura lent it to Annabel," she explained.

"No I didn't," said Laura, "I lent it to *you*."

"Laura – shut up," said Lucy.

Laura reached again and again for the book. Sebastian held it as high as he could, hooting with the sort of unkind laughter Annabel hadn't heard since primary school. Perhaps there was something to be said for going to a girls' school after all. It meant you didn't have

81

to put up with the behaviour which surfaced occasionally in every boy, however sensible, and always made girls look greater imbeciles than the boys themselves.

"*Please*, Sebastian," pleaded Annabel. "If Janet sees that book I'm in trouble."

"Poor liddle Barbie-Brain!" He dodged Laura, sprang over the wall and set off at a jog across the field. "Is Mommy gonna be real mad widd you?"

Before her brain could object, Annabel stepped into the field. "Just give me the book, will you?"

"Come and get it, then!"

She felt a stab of joy so deep it hurt. In spite of using her nickname with more hostility than any girl at school ever had, he was turning her attempt to retrieve the book into a pursuit of a different kind. He wanted her to chase him. He wanted her to catch him.

In the corner of the field by the stile he threw the book aside. It landed about two metres away, its garish jacket flapping in the grass. Annabel stopped, breathless. He lay down and tipped his cap over his eyes.

"Quick, Annabel, get the book!" called Lucy from the wall.

But Annabel approached slowly. She picked up the book. Sebastian didn't move.

"Are you asleep?" she asked, her heart beating very fast.

He didn't answer. She went closer. She could see his shirt moving up and down as he breathed. "You must be dead, then. I don't care, though, because I've got the book."

She knelt beside him, her dress spreading around her, feeling as reckless and free as the gypsy she half-believed Lucy to be. Suddenly, with one movement, he plucked the cap from his face and the book from her hand, and sprang up.

"No you haven't!" he cried, and set off again towards the cottage, not running very fast. They both knew the game was over.

Her heartbeat settling, Annabel stayed where she was, pulling up buttercups. She was used to being cautious, but she suspected she felt happy. Really happy, for the first time since Dad had moved out. Sebastian had teased her today, but he had also played with her. Most satisfying of all, he had talked to her. Just *her*, without Lucy elbowing her out of the way.

Janet and Frank had come back into the garden. Annabel wandered slowly across the field, tiny yellow petals dropping from her dress.

"Here, drink this," said Janet, handing Annabel a glass of lemonade with frozen plastic elephants floating in it.

Sean was leaning against the copper beech. He came and sat beside Annabel in its shade.

He didn't look at her, but she knew he was concerned that she might be upset. To reassure him she wasn't, she said, "Pink elephants! And she thinks *we're* children!" and drank a lot of lemonade in one slurp.

Two weekends ago, at the Horwell Scouts' Barbecue and Barn Dance, Sean had sat beside her in the shade of a tree, just like this. They'd been eating scalding, half-burnt corn cobs, but he'd only taken three bites before someone had called him away. Annabel had vented her disappointment on her corn cob, chucking it into the nearest bin. Later, she'd been thrilled when Mrs Turnbull, who was organizing the barn dancing, had pushed her into line opposite Sean, and his had been the first hand she'd touched.

It was only two weeks ago. And the embarrassing scene on the tennis club wall was only two *days* ago. But the things that had happened since then had pushed Sean further and further backwards until he was almost invisible.

Sebastian and Lucy were jumping over Janet's flower beds, giggling and shrieking. As Annabel watched, Lucy collapsed on her back and Sebastian pretended to stand on her stomach.

"Look at those two," said Laura. She drained her glass, throwing her head back. "I thought Americans were supposed to be sophisticated!"

"In the movies," said Sean dryly.

Annabel smiled. "Shall I get you another drink, Laura? Coke, was it?"

"He's a bit keen on himself, that Sebastian," said Laura, surrendering her glass. "Sean thinks so too. Don't you, Sean?"

Sean shrugged. He seemed embarrassed.

"He shouldn't have teased Annabel like that, should he?" insisted Laura.

Sean shrugged again. Annabel refilled Laura's glass, watching him. He'd definitely gone red.

"If you ask me," said Laura peevishly, "there'll be tears before bedtime."

Sean sighed. "Ignore her," he said to Annabel.

Annabel didn't say anything. She tightened the stopper of the Coke bottle and put it back on the tray. Suddenly, Laura took her elbow.

"Frank Houseman's secret life is all round the village, you know," she whispered. She was so close Annabel could feel her breath. "Is it true that he got an American girl pregnant when he was a student over there, and refused to marry her?"

Annabel stared at her, stunned. "No, of course it isn't true!"

"My dad says he wouldn't put something like that past him," said Laura lightly. Annabel had noticed before that her voice was at its

85

nicest when she was making the most mischief. "Dad says he's a cold fish. Doesn't he, Sean?"

"Stop drivelling," said Sean. He pushed back the front flap of his hair, looking at Annabel with sandy, speckled eyes. "You know she's been let out early for good behaviour, don't you?"

"It's not true, about Mr Houseman," declared Annabel. She wasn't sure what *was* true, but she couldn't leave Laura's assertion unchallenged. "He *did* marry her, and she wasn't pregnant – I mean, not until afterwards. But she died when Sebastian was a baby, and he's been brought up by her sister and brother-in-law in America. That's all."

"How did she die?" asked Laura eagerly, her eyes like marbles. "She didn't fall down the stairs in mysterious circumstances, did she? Or get murdered, like in *Rebecca*?"

"Oh, Laura, for goodness' sake," said Annabel, exasperated. "How can you say all this stupid stuff?"

"Don't worry, it comes to her quite easily," said Sean.

Laura let go of Annabel's elbow and pushed him petulantly. "You can talk. It was *you* who said it wasn't fair to expect Annabel to give up her whole summer to some boring Yank. You were moaning because you wouldn't be able to see her much. And don't deny it, I heard you with my own ears."

ONE SET TO LOVE

It was very, very hot at the tennis club. So hot that even though it was Sunday afternoon there were few players and no spectators. Annabel sat in the front row, the wooden bench burning the backs of her legs and the sun burning her face.

She was glad she'd brought her sun hat. She put it on and tucked her hair up underneath it. Her shoulders, which Janet had larded with sun block, sizzled under a sky painted by a five year old.

Sean and Laura were hitting practice balls to each other, not very expertly. When Laura did a shot so wild that the ball almost bounced over the wire netting surrounding the court, Sean smiled at Annabel. She smiled back tolerantly.

Sebastian came out of the changing room carrying three racquets, a box of balls, a towel and a water bottle. He was wearing the white baseball cap the wrong way round. The embroidered logo on his tennis shirt said "Belmont County Country Club". His legs were hairy, but not chimpanzee hairy, and his calves were knottier than Sean's. Annabel watched, squinting, as he collected some balls and took his place on the same side of the net as Laura.

"Hey, Sebastian!" called Lucy, rounding the corner of the clubhouse. "You're supposed to be playing on my side!"

"Who says?" Sean stopped bouncing a ball and stood with one hand on his hip. "We arranged that I was going to be your partner, didn't we?"

Lucy bounded on to the court, hitting the strings of her racquet against her palm. She'd put on a white headband, and although she didn't have a proper tennis dress like Laura, her shorts and T-shirt looked businesslike enough. "Don't be so possessive, Turnbull," she said.

"You just want to be on the winning side," Laura told her, with some perception. "Any American's bound to be able to play better than all of us."

"Girls, girls..." Sebastian took a coin from his pocket and flipped it expertly. "It's only a game. If Lucy wants to play as my partner, who cares? Come on, let's start. Sean, you call."

"Heads," said Sean, screwing up his eyes against the sun. Annabel liked the way Sebastian said "Sean", pronouncing it "Shon". It sounded softer, and properly Irish.

"Heads it is."

Laura was right. Sebastian could play better than all of them. He returned the first ball so aggressively that Laura yelped and jumped out of its way. His second return sped past Sean at eye level and hit the fence with a *thwack* like a cricket ball.

"What the hell are you doing?" Both Sean's hands were on his hips now. "That could have bloody well blinded me!"

"I'm playing tennis," said Sebastian calmly. "What are *you* doing?"

Annabel felt uncomfortable. She was glad she was too far away to intervene.

But Lucy hurried to the rescue. "You're really good!" she said to Sebastian, beaming encouragingly. "But we're not—"

"Why did you offer me a game, then?" Sebastian turned on Sean. "You told me you were getting coaching."

"Well, I am. From my dad."

Sebastian looked at the sky and tossed his racquet in the air. It fell with a crunch about a metre away. "Oh, great. From your dad. And he's a professional, I suppose?"

"Don't be silly." Laura couldn't leave her brother undefended. "He's just a club player, like everyone else. And you're lucky he signed you in, since you're not even a member."

Sebastian kicked the ground. "Look, I just wanted to play some tennis, so—"

"So lower your game," said Lucy steadily.

Annabel could tell they were all rattled. But although Sebastian's touch last night on her bare arm was historical fact, her reaction to his behaviour today was much more difficult to work out.

They began to play again. Sebastian *did* lower his game, slightly, but Laura and Sean had no real chance. And Lucy was left with nothing to do but run helplessly around while Sebastian scooped up all the balls and returned all the shots.

Without doubt, he knew how to play. He didn't fool around, or miss shots and swear, like everyone else at Broughton Tennis Club. His determination to win drove him to do his best with every ball, even against such useless opposition. Annabel saw his selfishness, but turned away from it.

At the end of the first set Lucy dropped her racquet and threw herself theatrically onto the dusty tarmac. Corkscrews of hair which had escaped her pony tail stood up all around her head. "Water, water!" she gasped. Annabel watched her, wondering how she managed to look attractive whatever she did, without looking unintelligent.

"Here." Sebastian smiled down at Lucy, offering her the water bottle. She sat up and drank, then Sebastian took the bottle, wiped the top and drank from it himself. Without offering it to anyone else he dried his face on the towel, cleared the net with a scissor-jump and went to the base line, twirling his racquet. "Second set!"

Lucy groaned and stood up. Laura, wiping her forehead on her wristband, dutifully took up her place on Sean's side of the net. But Sean, who had left the court and was sitting on the same bench as Annabel, though some distance away, didn't move.

"Come on, Sean, move your butt!" called Lucy.

Annabel wished she had the courage to talk mock-American too. Sebastian's accent made their English voices sound like Yorkshire versions of C3PO, the comic robot in *Star Wars*.

Sebastian was delighted with Lucy's tribute. "Attagirl, Lucy!" he yelled, punching the air.

"Get lost," said Sean.

Annabel looked sidelong at him. His smooth face with its sprinkling of freckles looked pink, though whether from heat or anger was hard to tell. He was tapping his heel nervously on the ground.

"Hey, what's up?" Sebastian came to the door of the court and scrutinized Sean. There was concern, but no sympathy in his face.

"You know what's *up*."

Annabel had never heard Sean snarl like that. One of Lucy's names for him was Milky Bar, because he was sweet in some patient, steadfast way that boys usually weren't.

"Come on, Sean," pleaded Laura, putting her podgy little fingers through the holes in the wire fence "We've got two more sets to play."

"Shut up." He stood up and began to walk back to the clubhouse. "I'm not playing any more. You girls will just have to play singles."

"Hey, Sean," began Sebastian, but he stopped when Sean whipped round, his fore-lock flying, and hit the nearest bench with the rim of his racquet.

"And you can shut up, too. Who the hell do you think you are? It's a big joke, isn't it, making us look like complete cretins?"

Sebastian coloured. But he was stubborn, and he wanted his game of tennis. He stood his ground, tapping his racquet against the toe of his shoe, facing Sean without flinching. "Don't be an asshole, Sean. What's the point of—"

"*Me?*" Sean took two strides towards the wire netting, his face blotched with fury. Laura stepped back in alarm. "*I'm* an asshole? It doesn't look like that from where I'm standing."

Annabel's heart began to thud. It was all right for the boys to tease the girls over Laura's silly novel. Neither of them minded that at all.

92

But Sebastian's ego wouldn't allow him to play for anything less than victory, and Sean's refused to buckle under the humiliation. Laughing at girls was one thing, but laughing at each other was much more serious.

Sebastian came through the door of the court. Sweat was running down his temples, gathering in front of his ears. "What's your point?" he said to Sean aggressively. "If you want to say something, say it. OK?"

Laura was standing behind Sebastian, looking worried. "Let's go home, Sean," she said. "I don't want to play any more now, either."

"Shut up," her brother told her fiercely. "And keep out of this." His head jerked, as if he wasn't quite controlling it. "You know what my point is," he said to Sebastian. "If you had any courtesy at all you'd just let us play for fun."

He took a step towards Sebastian. Laura let out a whimper. But Sean's resentment was too deep for retreat. "You may be American, and rich, and have professional coaching," he said, spitting the words out, "but you're a tosser. And I don't play tennis with *tossers*."

Lucy, who had been leaning uneasily against the fence during this exchange, could no longer keep quiet. If Sean had his champion in Laura, then she would be Sebastian's. She stood up straight, her fists clenched with the thumbs inside, and glared at Sean. "Don't you realize you're totally useless at tennis anyway, Turnbull?"

Sean's mouth opened and shut, but no sound came out.

"If you ask me," said Lucy pitilessly, "it's a miracle that Sebastian's lasted this long. You should be congratulating him on his patience, not calling him names!"

Annabel didn't know what to think. Her brain felt as if it had been split in half. When Sebastian had questioned her nickname, Sean had stood up for her. But now, if she stood up for him in return, how would it look to Sebastian? Would he think she didn't like him? She looked from one boy to the other as they stood there face to face, sweating with exertion and tension.

The truth was, she *did* like Sebastian. She liked him in a desperate, life-changing way. It was crazy, but meeting him in the silver tunnel seemed to have given her the opportunity, like the dancing princesses in the story, to transform her dull existence into a magical one. The old Annabel, whose heart used to somersault dangerously if Sean turned to look at her from the steps of the school bus, had disappeared. In her place stood the new model, polished to perfection, waiting on the invisible threshold of – dare she say it – love?

Trembling, she took her sun hat off and stood up. Her hair showered her shoulders.

Her legs squelched as they tore themselves away from the bench. She looked at Sean defiantly.

"Lucy's right." Her voice sounded unrecognizably clear. She was aware of the heat-shimmer on the tennis court, the bandbox brightness of the sun, the horror on Laura's face and the disbelief on Sean's. "Have you forgotten that Sebastian's our guest? He hasn't come thousands of miles to be treated like this."

Sean's breath came in little gasps. His face was red on the cheeks and pale on the forehead and chin. Annabel thought he had never looked less appealing. She wondered how she could ever have actually had *dreams* about going out with him.

"Oh, that's how it is, is it?" Sean pushed his hair out of his eyes with a flailing, miserable movement. "You just can't get enough of it, can you, Annabel? You're no better than the brain-dead female in that stupid book!"

Annabel was silent. She looked at the ground. There was a pain in the bottom of her chest, just above her stomach, as if she'd eaten too many strawberries. No one said anything. Then Sean spun on his heel and headed, almost running, for the clubhouse. Laura began to weep quietly. Lucy, her brown arm around Laura's white shoulders, pulled her onto the bench.

Sebastian dropped his racquet, took off his cap and wiped his face with it. "Well, he was pretty sore, wasn't he?" Then, when no one replied, "What's a tosser?"

SCARED

"He won't be there, Lucy."

"Why not? Where else has he got to go?"

Annabel and Lucy were leaning on the wall by the newspaper shop.

"He'll just stay at Cairncross, I expect," said Annabel. "He'll probably watch videos, or sunbathe, or something."

"Well, I think he'll come down to the yard and help his dad," insisted Lucy. "It makes sense, Barb."

"Don't call me that."

"Sorry."

Annabel didn't feel quite right. A screen had rolled down between her and Lucy. Although they couldn't see it, both of them knew it was there.

"Look, Luce, I just think it looks a bit – you know, *chasey*. As if we're running after him."

"Running after him? Are you joking?"

"Oh, Lucy…"

"You can run after him if you like," said Lucy in a clipped sort of voice. "But I'd rather *he* did the running, thanks very much."

"Don't be horrible to me, Lucy," pleaded Annabel. "I haven't done anything."

"And you're not *going* to do anything either, are you?" She turned away from the wall and leaned her elbows on it. "If you had your way we'd just sit at home all day, waiting. But life's too short, Annabel. If we want to see him we'll have to go and find him."

Annabel's discomfort increased. "But will he want to see us?"

"Of course he will! Why are you being so *dumb*? You saw the way he acted yesterday. He likes us."

Annabel nodded uncertainly. Her instincts told her that Lucy's indiscreet behaviour would end up backfiring, and she couldn't bear her friend to make a fool of herself. But equally unbearable was the prospect of her own plan failing, and Sebastian going home with a picture of *Lucy* in his wallet. The backs of her eyeballs burned. The trouble was, she wasn't shameless enough to borrow Lucy's tricks. She'd tried, but she just wasn't. "He's the kind of guy who likes a joke," Lucy was saying. "He likes to fool around."

"I know that, Lucy. He did a bit of fooling around with *me* yesterday, if you remember."

Lucy looked down the High Street.

"When he made me follow him into the field, I mean," added Annabel.

"When he *made* you follow him!"

"But he *did*, Lucy."

"Look." Lucy's head flicked back. There was a hard, dissatisfied look in her eyes. "Just stop taking him so seriously, will you? A guy like Sebastian likes girls who are good fun."

"Why do you keep calling him a *guy*? Are you trying to talk American?"

"You're as bad as old Milky Bar Turnbull," said Lucy, kicking the wall with the heel of her sandal. "He can't take a joke, either. What an incredible fuss to make because Sebastian's better at tennis than him!"

"Lucy..."

"He makes me sick, and I hope you really *have* gone off him."

Annabel was silenced.

"I don't care what you do, but I'm going down to Houseman's," declared Lucy, shaking out her curls. She had a short skirt on, with a little leather bag diagonally across her shoulder, and her gold ear-rings. She walked three steps, then looked back at Annabel. "Oh, come on, Barb. You can't let me go on my own."

Annabel tried not to think about the possibility of seeing Sebastian. She tried not to remember the sleepless heat of last night, when every time she'd closed her eyes a picture of him walking across the field in his loose-kneed way, with his hands in his pockets and the peak of his cap facing sideways, had forced them open again. She couldn't look at him in darkness, but she couldn't *not* look at him in daylight.

Perhaps Lucy was right. Life was too short to plan a plan for ever. In the end, you had to get on with carrying it out.

"All right, Luce. But if he's not there, *you* can explain to Frank exactly what we're doing barging into his yard."

Houseman's Feed and Seed yard had once been the courtyard of an inn. The inn had been demolished long ago, and shops with offices above them built on the site. But the old archway and the courtyard it led to had been left standing. Frank's business premises had been converted from the original stable block behind the cobbled yard.

Despite her indifference to the man himself, on the rare occasions when she'd had reason to go to his yard Annabel had liked it. She liked the smell of leather which hung about the large, low-beamed shop, and the chaotic office reached by an iron staircase outside the building. She liked to imagine the eighteenth-century stable boys climbing up the staircase to their straw beds, and the coaches trundling over the cobbles. She was a romantic moron, Lucy would say.

"Oh, Lucy, look!" she exclaimed as they entered the yard. "It's Jed!"

The spaniel was tethered to the iron banister. When he saw Annabel he pulled on the leash, his wet nose searching for her hand. "Good boy," she said soothingly, patting him. "Nice dog. You're hot, aren't you?" She looked up at Lucy. "It's Frank Houseman's dog. What's he doing here, I wonder?"

Lucy grasped her shoulder. "Sebastian must have brought him. I told you he'd be here, didn't I?"

It was lunchtime, and the yard was deserted except for Reg, who wore a brown overall and helped in the shop. He was standing in the doorway, taking the sun. "Can I help you, ladies?" he asked, showing his false teeth.

Annabel felt the little glow of recognition she always felt when she heard Reg speak. He sounded like her grandfather. She stopped patting Jed and stood up. "Er – has Sebastian – you know, Mr Houseman's son – been in today?"

Reg's face, which was the same colour as his overall, took on an alert look. He knows, thought Annabel. He knows the ruthlessness of Lucy's pursuit, and can see that she's pulling me along with her. "Upstairs in t'office yonder," he said, jerking his thumb towards the door at the top of the iron staircase. "Wanted me to go and get him some

101

sandwiches at t'pub, but I can't leave t'shop."

"Mr Houseman's not here, then?" said Lucy.

"No, lass. Out delivering Mrs Oliver's straw. Back about two," he said.

"Come on, Annabel," said Lucy, and put her foot on the first stair. But before Annabel could follow she was stopped by a familiar voice.

"Hey, girls!" Sebastian was leaning on the railings by the office door, wearing a loose white cotton shirt and no baseball cap. He was standing with his weight on one foot and the other on the lowest bar of the railings, leaning forward on his elbows, his forearms dangling in space, his fingers lightly interlocked. He looked perfect. Like a single, unimprovable brush-stroke.

"Hey," he said again as Lucy reached him. He was smiling his wide smile, looking more animated than Annabel had yet seen him. Dangling from his fingers was a bunch of keys. "You look cool."

Lucy's features disappeared behind a grin like the one the Cheshire Cat left behind. "Cool as in cool, or cool as in hot?"

Sebastian did something with his eyes which Annabel knew she wasn't supposed to notice. They widened and narrowed again in less than a millisecond. "Well, I wouldn't like to guess how *hot* you are, Lucy."

Annabel's labouring heart laboured more painfully. Listening to this exchange was as depressing as being with someone who'd had a glass or two of wine when she hadn't. No, it was worse, because Lucy was intoxicated with the very thing that Annabel herself wanted to drink.

"Recognize these keys, Annabel?" asked Sebastian, holding them up.

Annabel had seen them on the kitchen table at home, when Frank came to call. She began to feel uneasy. "They're your father's."

Sebastian held up each key separately. "This is the shop, and this is the office, and this is the store-room, according to my buddy Reg. This one's the farmhouse, and this one..." He held up what was obviously a car key, with its little electronic box. His teeth flashed gleefully. "Well, I guess this one must be the car."

Without warning, his free hand took hold of Lucy's. She gasped.

"How about taking a ride?" he asked, starting down the stairs. Lucy had no choice but to follow. "He's gone off in the delivery truck and left the rabbit parked right here in the yard. So what's to stop us?" He paused on the last step. "You're coming with us, aren't you, Annabel? To the beach?"

Annabel was nonplussed. She couldn't look at Lucy. "Yesterday you said your dad wouldn't lend you the car," she reminded

103

Sebastian. "We were talking about incapacitating him. Don't you remember?"

He looked at her calmly. "Well, that was yesterday, Barbie-Brain."

Reg had come out of the shop. "Thanks for telling me where these were, Reggie-boy," said Sebastian, waving the keys. "I'll get the car back in good time. Tell my dad not to worry."

"Right, lad," said Reg.

Annabel hated to see the old man, who had been a trusted and trusting employee since before Sebastian was born, treated so shabbily. She went to Sebastian, who had let go of Lucy's hand and was untying Jed. Hardly noticing what she was doing, she pulled the soft material of his shirt. "But when your dad finds you've taken the car, he's going to blame Reg for giving you the keys, isn't he?"

He stood up. Being so close to him made Annabel's skin prickle. "Look," he said patiently. "What's your problem? Wouldn't you rather spend the day on the beach than stick around this hole?"

Now the moment had come, the decision was surprisingly easy. Defending him yesterday when the alternative was to defend Sean Turnbull was different. Even in its delirious state Annabel's heart knew that to take his side today would be wrong.

"I'm not coming," she told him steadily. "And neither is Lucy. Are you, Lucy?"

104

Lucy was standing in the middle of the yard, like the only skittle left in a ten-pin bowling lane. The sun shot her hair with a thousand lights. Her fingers played a silent scale on the flap of the bag she wore on her hip. The screen between her and Annabel came down again, thicker than before.

"I don't see why not," she said bossily. "I'd like to go to Scarborough, even if you wouldn't."

Lucy and Annabel weren't allowed to go anywhere without telling their parents first. "Hadn't you better ask your mum?" asked Annabel in astonishment.

"What's the matter?" retorted Lucy. "Are you scared?"

Annabel *was* scared. She was scared to disobey her mother, scared to get into a car obtained under false pretences by a boy who'd never driven in England, and scared to admit that she was scared. Cold with dismay, and horrified at the way everything had gone so quickly and completely wrong, she began to walk towards the archway.

"Annabel – are you sulking?" called Lucy.

She didn't answer. She hurried through the black shadow thrown by the arch and opened the gate to the field by the river where the children's swings were. The playground was empty. It was too hot at this time of day for little children. Annabel walked quickly

105

towards the parents' bench under the ash tree. When she reached it, she sat down and put her head in her hands, pressing her fists into her eye sockets. Her head ached. But she couldn't go home because Janet would want to know what was the matter, and she couldn't tell her.

Not yet, anyway. Later, if Sebastian and Lucy hadn't come back by teatime, she would have to.

LIKE A NUN

Annabel hadn't seen Lucy or Sebastian for four days. To be truthful, she'd avoided them. She'd told Janet that the heatwave was making her so tired she'd rather stay indoors. And Sean and Laura's parents had taken them away on holiday, so she didn't have to see them either.

Quietly, while Janet was in the bath on Thursday evening, she got out the colour box and expensive brushes Dad had given her on her twelfth birthday. She filled a jam jar with water. She took the vase of broken geraniums off the kitchen windowsill and placed it in the middle of the table, and taped a piece of paper she'd been soaking in the sink to the drawing board. Then she dried it with her hair drier. When it was smooth she put two cushions on a chair, propped the board against the table, sharpened her pencils and began.

107

In her heart, she knew what she was doing. She was purifying herself. She was washing away all traces of childish resentment, so that she could present a squeaky-clean face to Dad's desertion of her. By the time he came back to Broughton for a visit her feelings would be starched, dried, ironed, aired, folded and put away in the drawer.

The geraniums would help her do it. Concentrating on drawing such complicated flowers, then painting their coral-reef colours, would leave no space in her brain for anything else. Dad always said watercolours were lively little devils, always running away when you thought you had them under control. Well, she wasn't going to allow her thoughts to do that.

What was the line in that book by some famous woman, which Mrs Phillips had once read from? Annabel had liked the line, and had repeated it to herself after Mrs Phillips had put the book away. "Like a nun withdrawing." That was it. She'd be like a nun withdrawing.

She would have to fold up her feelings about Sebastian, too, as secretly as a love letter. She would have to blank out every remembered sensation, and put away the picture of him leaning over the railing in Frank's yard, when she'd seen for the first time, with an artist's eye, how beautiful he was.

There was no doubt that she'd been stupid. Stupidity had made her persist in the infantile belief that Janet and Dad would get back together, and everything would be all right. It was stupidity which had made her not try at school and then resent Janet's anxiety about her progress. And it was stupidity of the grossest, blindest kind which had deluded her into thinking that Sebastian might like her.

Her only comfort was that he didn't seem to like anyone else either. Not his father, not Janet, not Sean. Not even Lucy, really. He was playing with her just like he was playing with everyone. He wound people up and watched them explode, or, in Annabel's case, disintegrate.

And as for Lucy…

Mr Alderson, Lucy's father, had waited at the cottage on Monday evening with Frank and Janet. He'd quizzed Annabel like a prosecution lawyer, asking her repeatedly to tell them *exactly* what Sebastian had said, *exactly* where he'd intended to take Lucy, *exactly* what time they'd driven off.

It had been scary. Especially when Lucy's mother had phoned at half-past nine to say that Lucy was back, and Frank, grabbing the receiver from Janet, had ordered Mrs Alderson to send Sebastian round to the cottage immediately, on foot. Annabel had been hurried out of the room when Sebastian arrived, but she'd sat on the stairs and listened to the argument between his father and Mr Alderson.

Mr Alderson had insisted that Sebastian explain himself, and Sebastian had refused, and Mr Alderson had asked him if he made a habit of abducting people's daughters. Frank's voice had demanded stiffly whether Mr Alderson thought his son was some kind of criminal, and Mr Alderson had retorted that if he was unscrupulous enough to take unauthorised possession of a car he was probably quite capable of taking unauthorised possession of a fifteen-year-old girl. At this point, Annabel had put her hands over her ears and gone slowly upstairs.

Janet had told her on Tuesday that Lucy was grounded for a week and Sebastian's aunt and uncle in America had been informed of his behaviour. Annabel had asked why, and Janet had explained, rather uneasily, that they seemed to be the only people Sebastian had any respect for. His respect for his father was so flagrantly absent that Frank couldn't work out how to punish him.

Janet bustled into the kitchen, dressed to go out. Her favourite ear-rings, brightly coloured enamel parrots, trembled as she swung her hair around her shoulders. Annabel saw the excitement on her face, and a vision came into her mind of Frank Houseman sitting at Sunday lunch with a glass of wine in his hand, smiling, his moustache twitching. *Could* a middle-aged, overweight woman in an

110

embroidered cheesecloth blouse be attractive?

"Annabel, you're drawing! Daddy would be so pleased!"

"I haven't called him Daddy since I was six, Janet."

"*Dad*, then," said Janet, dumping her handbag on a chair and searching it. "Is Lucy coming round tonight?"

Annabel went on drawing. "Lucy's grounded."

"Oh, of course she is. Would you like to go round to her house, then?"

"No."

Janet found her lipstick and began to apply it, stretching and pursing her lips at her reflection in her handbag mirror. "Someone told me that Americans call a handbag a purse," she said. "Or did I hear it in a film? Anyway, I wonder what they say when they really *do* mean a purse?"

She put the mirror and lipstick in her bag and went into the hall. Then she came back again. She stood by the window, blocking Annabel's light. "Frank's taking me for dinner at the Swallowdale Hotel," she told her. "I wish you could come too, sweetheart. You never seem to go anywhere."

She looked at Annabel fondly for a moment. "But you're probably happier sitting here painting, aren't you? You always were a quiet little thing. There's some cold ham and potato salad for your dinner, and I expect you to eat it. I know you girls, always worrying about your figures. What a joke!"

Annabel detected nervousness. She looked at her mother curiously. The evening light stroked the edges of Janet's profile, as if Annabel had drawn it with a soft pencil and rubbed the outline with her thumb. "I'll be all right, Janet," she said. "You just have a nice time and forget about me."

"We won't be late. Frank's left Sebastian alone in the house too." Her head turned so quickly that her hair spun, settling less smoothly. "Oh! Would you have liked to have him round, to keep you company, darling? *Rats*, we should have thought."

"It's all right," said Annabel. "Really, I don't want anyone."

So it was all right to leave Annabel alone with Sebastian, though he couldn't be trusted with Lucy. The only comfort Annabel could draw from this was that it proved her theory. However much Janet looked at her, she never saw what was really there. She saw the little girl in the photo on the mantelpiece, with tiny square teeth and a frill round her swimsuit.

Janet began to walk about restlessly. "Did you hear a car, baby?"

"No."

"Frank's never late. He's always telling me off about punctuality." She compared her watch with the electric clock. "It's not twenty-five past seven yet, is it? The table's booked for eight. Are you sure you'll be all right?"

"I'm sure. Look, why don't you go into the sitting room, so you can watch for the car and run out when it arrives?"

Janet laughed. It was a forced, trilling sort of laugh. "Annabel! You make me sound like some mooning adolescent. It's only Frank, you know."

"Anyone at home?" said a voice in the hall.

Everyone in Broughton left their front doors open. Frank came in with a gift-wrapped box under his arm, smiling nervously. "For you, madam," he said to Annabel, with a little bow.

Annabel looked at Janet, who nodded encouragement. She looked happy. She looked really *happy*. Annabel's heart began to murmur suspiciously. "Why have you brought me a present?" she asked Frank. "It's not my birthday."

"Go on," he said, his smile growing in confidence. "Open it."

It was a box of chocolates. Expensive ones, not from Mrs Evans's newsagents, whose stock Annabel knew well.

She felt shy. Frank Houseman hadn't given her a second glance, much less a box of chocolates, until a week ago. She looked down at the tastefully decorated package in her hands, realizing that it didn't really have much to do with her, or with Janet. It had a lot to do with her dad, who wasn't even there, and whose absence, she realized with a flash of insight, was a gift too.

As she set the box of chocolates down, she looked with new eyes at the man who had given them to her. Shyness turned to dismay. Butterflies flapped in her stomach, and her breath shortened. Tears waited behind her eyes. "Janet –" she began.

Concerned, Janet put her arm around her. "What is it, darling? Don't you like the chocs?"

"Oh, Janet – it isn't the *chocs*!" Annabel pushed her mother away. "Don't you see? I'm not a child. Don't you hear? I – am – not – a – *child*! Why do you never tell me anything?"

Bewildered, Janet looked to Frank for help. He was leaning against the worktop with his arms folded. "How do you mean, lass?"

"She never tells me the truth," said Annabel, the tears coming. "All this stuff happens, but she keeps it secret, as if I'm too dim to understand."

Frank didn't protest, or tell her off. His smile, which had diminished, returned to the corners of his mouth. His features looked less sharp-edged than usual. Annabel, seeing Sebastian's ghost in his face, pressed her hand over her heart in a vain effort to stop it hurting.

Janet tried to speak, but Frank signalled to her. "What stuff?" he asked Annabel. "Come on, now you've started we might as well hear the rest."

"Sebastian." The word – so special, so full of things that no one else knew about – came out like a cough. "He got here last Friday, didn't he? And you both knew he was coming long before that. But why did no one tell *me* until Sunday morning, when he'd already been invited to lunch? So that Janet could present him like some sort of – of – centrepiece for her table?"

"Annabel!" Janet was staring at her. "Don't be so silly. And anyway, you told me you'd met him already, when you were going for a walk or something."

Frustration threatened to overwhelm Annabel. She closed her eyes and tried to breathe. "Janet, for God's sake *listen*, will you, and try to understand?"

"But—"

"Go on, Annabel," interrupted Frank. "Let's hear what you've got to say."

Annabel paused. She was losing her nerve. "I don't know what I *have* got to say. It's just this secrecy – over Sebastian, and over what's going on with—"

She remembered just in time who she was talking to, and stopped.

"With me, do you mean?" asked Frank. He

was looking at her steadily, with his eyebrows raised in the middle and drooping at the sides.

"Yes, I suppose so."

There was a hollow, detached sort of silence. Annabel could hear the swish, swish, swish of a lawn sprinkler in a nearby garden. Then Frank took Janet's hand.

"I agree with you, Annabel," he said unexpectedly. "I believe in straight talking. It's Janet who thinks you need to be protected."

Annabel looked at Janet's small, square hand in Frank's bony one. It was her left hand, but she hadn't put her usual rings on it. Annabel absorbed this, then looked at Frank's face. "Protected from what?"

"Well, from worrying, like, and building things up in your mind. Janet says you're the kind of child – sorry, I mean the kind of *person* who does that. So she wanted to sort things out first, then let you know what you had to know after."

He glanced at Janet, who nodded. His grasp on her hand tightened.

"And you're not the only one who'd never heard about Sebastian, you know. People round here made it clear they didn't like him being brought up in America. To be honest, I felt a bit of a lemon, and kept quiet about it. After a while, people stopped asking after him." He stroked his moustache, looking at Annabel out of the corners of his eyes. "It's all right, I know what sort of gossip's flying around Broughton, courtesy of Mrs Evans. But there's no dark secret. It was a hasty decision, but I've never regretted it. The boy's got a great life over there."

This was the most Annabel had ever heard Frank Houseman say. Taciturn, people called him. Laura's dad thought he was a cold fish. But here he stood with her mother's hand in his, telling her the truth at last.

"You know what I'm going to say now, don't you?"

Annabel's legs felt weak. She leaned against the back of the chair.

"Look at me, lass," said Frank gently.

She looked at him. She looked at Janet too. On their faces was a message so clear she wondered how she could ever have accused Janet of secrecy or Frank of coldness.

"We were going to tell you tomorrow, when Janet could show you her ring." His voice was calm, but he couldn't keep pride and satisfaction out of it. His hand went to the pocket of his jacket. "It's still in its box," he said to Janet, "but I might as well give it to you now."

"No, don't!" cried Annabel.

Something had struck her, with the force of the freezing sea at Scarborough which she and Dad used to run into, yelling. She laid her hand on Frank's sleeve. "Leave it where it is. I don't want to see it."

117

The truth stared at her.

Sebastian would always be the boy who had shown her the way into that magic garden. But when Janet and Frank were married, he would be her *brother*.

"Annabel..." Janet was near to tears. "Please, baby..."

But Annabel's misery was too deep for courtesy or compassion. She stumbled to the door, wondering where her legs had gone. She knew she was in the hall because she could see the grandfather clock, and Janet's raincoat hanging on the stand. She reached out for the banister-post, but it turned to nothingness beneath her fingers.

"Oh no," she thought as the stairs rose to meet her face. "How can this be happening to me?"

GROUNDED

It was the following afternoon. Annabel guessed it was about four o'clock. She'd been sitting for a long time on the garden wall, wishing as hard as she could that Dad would cross the field, grinning and waving. Her need for him to come home and sort things out was so strong it made her stomach hurt.

Maybe wishing wasn't enough. If only she believed in God, she could pray. She looked at the trees behind the field, and the hazy sky. Maybe you didn't have to believe in God. Maybe if your need was great enough the power of the need overcame your lack of faith, and God would answer the prayers even of an unbeliever.

"Dear God," she murmured uncertainly. "If you can hear me, please try to help me. Please send my father back to me."

It didn't seem to be doing any good.

She wandered into the field, trying not to remember the scene it had witnessed last Sunday over *The Dreamboat of Firewater Lake*. Tomorrow, when Janet made her usual Saturday morning trip to Horwell Public Library, perhaps she'd go with her and visit the fiction department.

The weather was still very warm, and humid too. Annabel went through the kissing gate on the other side of the field and down the path which led to Broughton High Street. Careless of her appearance, she was wearing a sun-bleached divided skirt and a sleeveless T-shirt which didn't match it, and her old flip-flop sandals. Her hair was scraped viciously into a pony tail, secured with one of Janet's Indian scarves.

Try as she might, she couldn't help thinking about Sebastian. By now he would know that the girl whose personality justified her nickname was soon to be his sister. What was he thinking?

As she reached the bottom of the hill the phone box on the corner of Lucy's street came into view. It was exactly a week since the two girls had stood there in the evening sunshine and discussed the boy shortage. That evening, Lucy had made her laugh.

Oh, Lucy, *please*, she begged silently. I don't really want to be a nun withdrawing. And who else can help, since Dad's not here? Who?

120

When she rang the doorbell an upstairs window opened and Lucy's head appeared. "Annabel!" she exclaimed in astonishment.

Annabel couldn't speak, but smiled.

"Don't go away!" cried Lucy. She slammed the window, ran downstairs and opened the front door. "Come in, Barb – oh, sorry!"

"It doesn't matter." Annabel had thought about a lot of things while painting the geraniums. "I think I got a bit over-sensitive about that."

Lucy's smile was relieved, but her eyes were serious. "I'm never going to call you that again. And if I don't, no one else at school will either. Now come in and tell me all the news."

They went into the cool sitting room. Lucy flipped open the venetian blinds. "My mum says the sun fades the carpet. But we can't sit in the dark, can we?"

Annabel looked round the room, with its fragrant flower-arrangements and neat, welcoming atmosphere. She sighed, feeling a sense of loss.

"Mum's at work, and Dad's gone on a golfing weekend in Scotland," said Lucy. "Mum hates golf, of course, so she refused to go. I wanted to see what Scotland's like, but they wouldn't let me go because I'm grounded. Not fair, is it?"

Annabel sat down on the arm of the sofa. "Lucy…"

"Would you like a cold drink? Or coffee? We've got raspberries from the garden for tea. Perhaps there's enough for you to stay and share them. I'll just look in the fridge, shall I?" She was already halfway to the door.

"Lucy!"

Lucy stopped, looking sheepish. She twisted her fingers together like she did when she was being presented with something in Assembly. Annabel noticed that her shoulders were high and her elbows stuck out. Her face was pale.

"Stop rabbiting and sit down," said Annabel. "I don't want anything."

Lucy walked back across the room and sat on the window seat, drawing her legs up underneath her. The slow-motion moment allowed Annabel to think.

"Are you surprised to see me?"

Lucy didn't reply. She looked out of the window. This length of silence was so unusual that Annabel began to feel concerned. She wondered if Lucy might be crying. But when her head turned her eyes were dry.

"You've avoided me for the whole week, haven't you?" she asked accusingly. "You knew I was grounded, but you didn't even phone me."

Annabel was taken aback. It was true, she *had* avoided her. But it was also true that Lucy hadn't phoned her, either. She decided to tell the truth. "I'm sorry, but I thought you'd phone *me*. When you'd calmed down."

Lucy's dark eyebrows came together. "What do you mean, when I'd calmed down?"

"Nothing."

Annabel hadn't meant to upset her friend, but at the back of her mind she wasn't surprised that she had. Lucy's relief that Annabel hadn't deserted her for ever had been genuine, but the grievance which festered under the surface had lost no time in revealing itself.

"You must mean something, Annabel. Come on, tell me."

Annabel sighed.

"And don't *sigh* like that!"

Annabel felt uncomfortable. She wondered why she was being accused of something, when it was Lucy who had misbehaved. "Look, Lucy," she said, as neutrally as she could. "Let's not quarrel about what happened on Monday. We quarrelled then, and one quarrel's enough, isn't it?"

The striped sunlight behind Lucy had turned her curls gold at the edges. Her eyes glittered. "What have you been doing all week?"

"Nothing," said Annabel truthfully. "Absolutely nothing."

"Haven't you been anywhere?" Lucy had started to twist her fingers again.

"No, nowhere," said Annabel. She thought. "Well, down to the newsagent's and the chemist. And into Horwell once on the bus, to

123

go to the Building Society. But nothing very exciting. Janet's been busy at the Women's Aid shop all week. And talking of Janet—"

"For God's sake!" The suspicion in Lucy's voice had turned into exasperation. "Stop acting so innocent, will you? Why bother to make up such stories?"

Annabel was so amazed her mouth actually fell open. She closed it again, but couldn't speak.

"I know who you've been with all week," said Lucy miserably. Her eyes filled suddenly, and she sniffed. "But I just wish I knew what you've been doing with him, that's all."

There was the kind of pause during which Janet always said three hundred more Chinese babies had been born. Or was it one hundred and three? Annabel's heart bulged. She put a hand on the back of the sofa to steady herself.

Lucy was jealous. *Lucy* was actually jealous of *her*.

"Do you think I've been with Sebastian?"

Lucy's tears overflowed. She couldn't speak. Shoulder-shaking sobs came, with hiccups in between. Annabel stared.

"Lucy – really and truly, I haven't. I didn't even *want* to see him."

"Rubbish!" Lucy's eyes flashed. "Don't lie to me, Annabel, I can't stand it."

"Lucy, I swear—"

"It's pathetic, the way you've been trailing

124

about after him. It's just *pathetic*!"

Annabel realized at last that reasoning with Lucy wasn't going to work. And telling her about Frank's proposal would only encourage her to step up her campaign to captivate Sebastian, with even less regard for Annabel's feelings than she'd already shown. Annabel's stomach tied itself into a hard knot. Feeling suddenly furious, she abandoned protest.

"*I've* been trailing about after him? *I'm* pathetic? What about *you*?"

Lucy stopped sniffing and stared at her.

"Yes, *you*, Lucy! It was *you* who chucked yourself all over Sebastian like – like a bucket of water!" Annabel wasn't sure that this had come out exactly right, but Lucy didn't try to interrupt. "The way you behaved in Brown's last Saturday was totally *gross*. And as for the worry you caused your parents, just so that you could show Sebastian off to a load of Scarborough trippers! Who do you think you're fascinating?" She stole this sarcastic question from Janet. "Not Sebastian, and not me either!"

Lucy got off the window seat and stood in the middle of the carpet, her fists clenched into tight white balls, with the thumbs inside as usual. The passion in her eyes was too intense for tears. "Annabel Bairstow, I hate you!" She hadn't said this since they were seven years old. "It's completely obvious that he likes *me* best! You may be pretty, Annabel, but you're boring, boring, boring!"

Annabel felt the blood drain away from her cheeks. She wondered if she was going to faint again.

"And I'll tell you another thing, shall I?" Lucy's nose was running. She pinched it impatiently. "He was *glad* you walked off in a huff like that. He said, 'Well, that's got rid of Barbie-Brain!' So there!"

Annabel put her hands over her ears. If Lucy was prepared to behave childishly, then so was she. Amazingly, Lucy took two strides towards her and wrenched her hands away. "No, you don't. You sit there and listen while I tell you what happened when he and I got into that car."

Annabel was sure she was going to be sick. But Lucy was like a robot, standing in front of her, holding her wrists with a hard, stinging grip. "We didn't go to Scarborough after all. We went to Haworth. Sebastian said you'd mentioned it was where some famous writers lived. I told him you must have read that in a tourist brochure. You've never heard of the Brontës, have you? Famous writers, indeed!"

Annabel tried to withdraw her hands, but Lucy's fury was strong. "He's educated, Annabel. He hasn't wasted his time at school like you have. We went to the Brontë museum, and he told me more about them in ten minutes than you could learn in ten years."

"Shut up, Lucy, just shut up!" Annabel was very angry, and her wrists hurt. "I don't care!" She did care, very much. "I don't care if Sebastian's the brainiest boy in the world – you may think he likes you, but I bet he laughs at you behind your back as much as he laughs at me! *I* met him first, Lucy, and he's *mine*!"

Lucy let go of her wrists. For a terrifying moment Annabel thought she was going to slap her. She put her hands instinctively in front of her face. But Lucy just stood there, her face still wet with tears, her breath rushing in and out noisily.

Annabel stood up, shaking a little, and walked to the door. Without looking back she left the house, and when she reached the street she started to run.

POWERED FLIGHT

She didn't stop running, all the way up the hill.

While she'd been in Lucy's house a gusty little wind had blown up. The white sky was greying from the west, and the air felt much less humid. The whole familiar landscape seemed touched by a dark, urgent mood.

She paused at the top of the hill, breathing fast, pressing her hands to her chest. She looked at the inscrutable face of the cottage. Lucy's words hurt too much to think about. Instead, she thought about Janet and Frank.

Their selfishness was scarcely credible. Without any sort of discussion, Janet had landed Annabel with a stepfather whose son's existence had embarrassed him for the last seventeen years. And if he didn't love his real son, how could he possibly love – or even tolerate – his stepdaughter?

Even Dad, in his attempts to be unselfish

towards Janet, had turned his back on Annabel. He wasn't here when she needed him most. And even if he had been, how could he possibly understand the significance of Sebastian's suddenly-altered status?

Love was supposed to be so wonderful. Films and books and songs said so. But in reality love was awful. Truly *awful*.

It only worked if the person you loved fell in love with you too. Like Romeo and Juliet. You never heard about Romeo and the girl down the street who never took any notice of him. Only Juliet, because she loved him back.

It wasn't fair, it just wasn't *fair*.

She began to run again. Past the cottage and along the main road towards Horwell. Running made her feel better, as if doing physical violence to herself stopped her doing mental violence. Her pony tail lashed the back of her head. Her sandals slapped the ground. *Slap, slap, slap.*

When she got to the silver tunnel she swerved under the archway without stopping. The breeze was rustling the birch leaves. The air was cooling fast. The stones beside the stream dented her thin soles, hurting her feet. As she slowed to a walk the first drop of rain fell on her forehead. Then another, on her bare shoulder. And another on the tip of her nose.

She put her arms round one of the slim silver trunks and lifted her face. The rain was coming faster and faster. It welded her fringe to her brow and her vest to her shoulders. It started to make puddles and rivulets between the stones, splashing over her feet.

This was the place where she'd first seen Sebastian, when he'd appeared from nowhere and cut her life to pieces.

She hugged the tree trunk tighter, screwing up her eyes. If she cried it wouldn't matter, because her tears would just get mixed up with the rain. But she didn't want to cry. She thought about how Lucy had sobbed, and told her she hated her. She thought about how Sean had hit the bench in fury. She remembered the bewilderment in Mr Alderson's voice.

Sebastian had caused jealousy between girls and rivalry between boys, and friction between adults. And in that moment of savage rage, when Lucy was holding her wrists, Annabel had felt the deepest agony of all. Whatever Sebastian did, her feelings about him hadn't diminished. If anything, they'd grown.

Four days of trying to be a nun hadn't worked. She still wanted Sebastian to love her. She wanted him to look at her, and smile, and put on silly voices to make her laugh. She wanted him to touch her, and although being kissed by boys hadn't been much fun so far, she was sure she wanted him to kiss her.

Love changes everything, Janet always said.

Well, she was absolutely right. Last Friday, when Annabel and Lucy had dawdled home in the evening sunshine, Annabel had had some sort of life, despite having to live it in boy-starved Broughton. Now, instead of turning it to gold as she'd hoped, love had smashed it to smithereens.

The downpour had become a torrent. Far away, Annabel heard the crack of thunder. She opened her eyes and waited. There was an almost imperceptible electric flash, and a few seconds later another, nearer bolt of lightning. She wasn't scared, though. She let go of the trunk, possessed by a feeling which definitely wasn't fear, and definitely wasn't self-pity. It was the opposite, in fact.

Astonishingly, it was power.

Strength flowed into her arms and legs. She leapt down the bank to the stream. She kicked off her sopping sandals without noticing where they fell. She didn't care if the thunderstorm broke the world into a million pieces, because she was stronger than any thunderstorm. If something was shattered, you put it back together again. Everyone knew that.

She splashed between the boulders, head down, searching. Janet's Indian scarf, reduced to a sodden rope, flapped against the side of her face. She tore it out of her hair and dropped it where she stood, and went on searching the ground.

She pounced like a tiger on a boulder which lay just beneath the surface. It was heavy, and she had to use both hands. Breathing heavily, she dislodged it and rolled it, over and over, until she'd got it onto the bank. Then she went back for another, and another. Different sizes, different shapes, rolling and dragging them to the flat place she had chosen.

They were wet and hard to handle, and tore her fingernails. They rolled over her bare feet and grazed them. But she felt no physical pain. Some force inside her was driving her beyond normal behaviour. Ignoring her streaming hair and dripping clothes, she collected more and more stones, laying them carefully on the ground in a pattern. Large ones, then smaller ones. Smooth ones, then jagged ones. Then she knelt down on the bank of the stream and scooped up handfuls of mud.

She began to work on the stones. She rolled the largest ones into position and pressed them into the soft earth. Then she fitted smaller ones on top of them, cementing them with mud, and stood back and looked at what she'd done. Then she took some of them away again and chose others to put in their place. At first it looked like a pile of stones, but as she worked excitement mounted in her heart. Was it slowly starting to look like – possibly – a lying-down horse?

The thunderstorm passed and the rain lessened, and still Annabel worked. It wasn't like painting geraniums on a piece of paper. It was more like the geraniums themselves. Three-dimensional. Real. She could touch the stone horse just like she could touch geraniums or any other object in the real world. Some distant words of Dad's came back to her. "There's no need to sneer at people who say things like 'I don't know much about art, but I know what I like'. That might be a cliché, but it's perfectly correct. Find what you like, and do it as well as you can."

She had found what she liked. Her imagination knew what it wanted. Her hands had done it. And now her eyes saw it. The horse lay there by the stream, where before there had been an empty space. With no help from anyone else, little Barbie-Brain Bairstow had created something from nothing.

Incredulous, she stood back.

"Annabel?" said a bewildered voice from the trees. "What in holy hell do you think you're doing?"

ON THE ROCKS

When Annabel heard Sebastian's voice she let out a sound somewhere between a gasp and a snort, and whipped round, her wet hair slapping her face. Horror and fury gathered inside her. Then a volcanic eruption of joy wiped them out.

"This is my horse!" she exclaimed, spreading her arms. "I made it!"

"Annabel, are you OK?"

She dropped her arms. She felt exhausted. "Of course. Are *you* OK?"

"Sure."

"Has your dad told you the news?"

"Yep." He was frowning, but without impatience. "Look at you!"

Annabel looked down. There were scratches on her arms and a large, discoloured graze on the instep of her right foot.

"What were you thinking of?" he asked.

"Coming all the way up here and – and – building a horse? With stones?"

It was true. In time-honoured Yorkshire fashion, she'd used the stones which lay around naturally. But it wasn't building. It was *sculpting*. What she'd made wasn't a wall, or a sheepfold, but a work of art. The pile of mud and boulders had become a horse lying on its side, with its forelegs tucked up in front of its chest and its head stretched on the ground as if asleep, or dead.

She sat down on a flat rock at the edge of the stream, shivering. "Where are my shoes?"

Sebastian took off the old waterproof jacket he was wearing and held it out. "Here, put this on. It belongs to my dad, but it'll keep you warm until you get home."

"I'm not going home," she said, not taking it. "I want to stay here for ever and ever."

Her teeth were chattering. She buried her toes in the mud and clasped her filthy hands, trying to brace her body.

"Come on, Annabel, it's getting late." He put the coat around her and crouched down on the bank. "My dad won't even notice I've left, but you don't want Janet to worry, do you?"

"I don't care what Janet thinks," she said. She drew the coat more closely around her shoulders. "I only care about my dad."

Sebastian looked interested. "Is your dad

135

still here, in Broughton? I mean, where is he?"

Carefully, with weak, trembling hands, she squeezed the seaweed strands of her hair. The landscape swam around her in a watery haze. Her limbs were no longer battery-charged. She felt as if she was drifting in an abandoned boat without sails or oars. "He lives in London," she said. "He moved there last week."

Because he was crouching lower than she was sitting, Sebastian saw her downcast eyes fill with tears. His face changed. "You're grieving for him, aren't you? Though he isn't even dead?"

She'd never thought of it in those words before, but he was right. She nodded.

"What's he like?" he asked gently.

"Well…" She felt uncertain. She was aware of his concern, without understanding it.

"Is he a farmer, like my dad used to be?" he prompted.

She shook her head. A sharp pain stabbed her temples. "His family were farmers, and wanted him to be. But he was more interested in designing buildings." She pressed her fingers to her forehead.

"So what happened?"

The pain in her head was strong. She swallowed, trying to relax. "When my grandad died, Dad sold the farm and put the money into his building business. But he's a self-taught artist, you see, and he teaches me, too.

136

He's always encouraged me, and bought me paper and paints. I never knew that I could make sculptures, though. He'll be amazed when I tell him about the horse."

"Will you go and see him in London?" he asked.

She shrugged. Her shoulders felt very small in the enormous coat, which was too big even for Sebastian. "I don't know. It costs a lot to get there."

"Well, my dad has money. More than you'd think."

Tears still threatened, but she fought them off. "I don't want—"

"I mean, he'll pay the train fare to London for you, I'm sure."

The tears spilled over. But she had to say what she felt, whatever the consequences. "No, he won't. He won't take any more notice of me than he has of you. I don't want him to be my dad. I just want my real dad."

Sebastian was silent. Annabel was too wet and cold and miserable to worry about whether she'd offended him. But when he sat down on a boulder beside her, he said something quite unexpected.

"Look, Annabel. Doesn't it occur to you that I have a real mom, just like you have a real dad?"

She stared at him, tears clinging to her eyelashes.

"At least your dad's around, and you can talk to him," he said. "He knows about my father and Janet. But my mom's dead, so how can I talk to her about it?"

She went on staring at him. Was it really possible to be possessive about someone who was dead?

His colour rising a little, he rested his elbow against his knee and put his hand over his cheek. "I guess it sounds nuts," he confessed. "But when my dad told me I just kind of – I don't know, I just flipped or something."

"What did you do?"

"I screamed at him." He looked into the trees, remembering it. "I thought he was going to land one on me, he was so mad. Maybe I said some stuff I shouldn't have. But *I* was mad too. I thought, what about Nancy? That's my mom. Doesn't he have any feelings? Dammit, it wasn't her fault she got killed."

He picked up a stone and hurled it into the water with all his strength. Watching him, Annabel tried to speculate why his father's re-marriage should mean so much to him, when his real family life was in California, with people who adored him. But the effort was too much, and made her head hurt.

She drew in her breath. He turned to look at her. Her tears were evaporating, leaving tight, salty patches on her cheekbones. "Well, at least you didn't faint, like I did. Your dad had to pick me up off the floor."

His eyes widened.

"I tried to rush upstairs, but I only got as far as the hall before I collapsed. I felt such a fool when I woke up on the sofa, with Janet crying and your dad looking at his watch because he'd booked a table at an expensive restaurant."

There was a pause, and then Sebastian's question edged warily into the silence. "Did they – did they go to the restaurant, even after you fainted and all?"

She nodded.

"Didn't Janet want to stay home with you?"

She gave him a soulful look. "Janet can't resist a slap-up meal, whatever happens. Once she saw I was all right, she was as ready to go as Frank was."

He thought hard for a moment, staring at nothing. Then he threw another stone into the stream. His voice was very quiet. "They had it all planned before I came over here, didn't they? They wanted me to get to know you and Janet, so that I'd accept the bombshell when they dropped it."

Annabel knew it was true. She blinked away the last tears. "They've treated us both like—" Looking around for an example, she alighted on the stone horse. "Like animals. Janet never tells me anything."

"Well, my dad doesn't tell me anything,

either," he said glumly. He picked up a stone, but didn't throw it. "He's never told me about the road crash which killed my mom, for instance. He doesn't mention it, ever." He paused. The stone dropped from his fingers. "In fact, he doesn't even mention *her*. He acts like she never existed."

"Haven't you asked him about her?"

"Come on, Annabel, you know what he's like."

"But she was your mother!"

He looked at her exasperatedly. "This is a man who abandons his son and forgets he ever had a wife. Do you think he has any *feelings*?"

She considered. Frank's dismissal of Sebastian was certainly strange. In comparison, Janet's behaviour was almost normal. "I feel like I've lost my father," she said slowly. "But although Janet can be impossible sometimes, at least she's always there. And she's completely predictable, like a Mars bar or something."

She saw his eyelids flicker, and hurried to comfort him. "Mind you, she's disappointed in me because I'm boring, like she thinks my dad is. She's managed to get rid of him, but she can't exactly send me back where I came from."

There was a silence, during which his gaze drew level with hers again. She let him look at her, aware that her fringe was drying in the

140

wisps Janet always said made her look like a toddler, listening to a story after its bath. She hoped Sebastian wouldn't think she looked like a toddler.

"Listen, Annabel…" Blacker than ever in the disappearing daylight, his eyes glowed with a sudden idea. "What are you going to do with the horse?"

It was very dark beneath the trees, but the clumpy outline of the stone horse was visible beside the stream. Already, some of the mud Annabel had used to cement it had fallen away. She sat there, hunched up in the coat, wondering what was in Sebastian's mind. "It'll be all right here," she said. "It belongs here, with the other stones. It's part of the landscape."

"But what if some kid comes along and kicks it to pieces?"

The thought amused her. "He'll get a very sore toe!"

"But—"

"Don't worry. The horse came from in here." She thumped her chest gently. "I can easily make something else. I can make whatever I like."

"Sure you can. But *where*? Right here by the stream?"

Her heart folded with dismay. He was quite right. What was the use of being able to make sculptures if you had nowhere to do it?

"I need a place to work, don't I?" she said. "And materials. I need things I can't possibly have." Her chin sank on to her chest. "Why am I so stupid?"

Sebastian laid his hand on the sleeve of the overcoat, close to her wrist. It was the first time he'd ever deliberately touched her. "Listen to my idea," he said. "Are you listening?"

She nodded.

"Have you ever been to Cairncross?"

She shook her head.

"Well, it's a pretty crazy place. The kitchen's less modern than Wilma Flintstone's. And the bathroom ... believe me, you don't want to hear. I'm not surprised your mom doesn't visit my dad there. But in the garden, there's a gazebo – a glass structure, for keeping people warm and dry while they look at a view. There's a lot of fancy ironwork on it, and it has a dome on top. It's neglected, like everything else, but it still has its roof, and if it leaks a bit we can put some plastic sheeting over it or something."

"Gazebo," she said, liking the sound of the word. Then she repeated it slowly, so as not to forget it. "Ga-ze-bo."

Sebastian let go of her arm. He was gazing at her with expectation. "The thing is, Annabel, it faces in all directions, and it's on the top of a hill. Don't you see? It can be light

142

all day. If my dad lets us fix it up, you could work in there, couldn't you? Would you like that?"

"Oh!" she gasped.

"It would be your ... studio."

"That would be wonderful!"

The gazebo *did* sound wonderful, and her desire not to disappoint Sebastian was very strong. But there was a more realistic consideration. "What would I do about getting materials, though? Clay, and so on?"

He seemed to be ready for this. "Your dad encourages you, you said. So let him find some encouragement in his wallet."

She thought about it. It was ages since Dad had bought her any painting things. Or anything at all, really. "I'm not sure. It's a bit difficult, since—"

"Look, why don't we see what my father says about the gazebo first?" he suggested. "The materials problem might sort itself out later."

"Do you think so?"

She looked at the water, which flowed very fast now over the boulders. Her heart contained so many feelings she couldn't sort them out. She was grateful for Sebastian's attempt to help her, and affected by the fever of his excitement, and overwhelmed by her attachment to him.

"It's a fantastic idea," she said, sincerely but

a little awkwardly. "And if your dad says no, well – thanks for thinking of it, anyway."

With her bare feet tucked up under the coat and her hair spread about her shoulders, she felt like a mermaid sitting on a rock. In fact, the whole setting was as unreal as a Scandinavian fairy tale. She was aware of the dripping trees, and the gurgling stream, and the bluish light between the silver birches.

"Look, it's getting pretty late." Sebastian's voice caressed the words with soft, half-swallowed American consonants. Listening to it, Annabel ached, physically, for him not to go back to the faraway place where everyone else talked like that too. "Don't you know where you left your shoes?"

"No."

"I'll go look for them."

He found the mud-sodden sandals on the other side of the stream. "Why don't you put them on and I'll take you home." He laid them beside her rock. "Is this your scarf?"

She uncurled her legs and slipped the thongs of the sandals between her toes.

"They're ruined," she said, looking at them ruefully. "And the scarf belongs to Janet. She'll kill me." Then she remembered something which stabbed her coldly, without any warning, in the middle of her chest. She turned away from him. "I can get home by myself, thanks."

144

"No you can't. Look at that foot. And it's getting dark."

She slid off the rock. "Really, there's no need."

"Are you ashamed to be seen with me, or something?"

"No, of course not."

"I mean, you're almost my sister, aren't you? I have to take care of you."

When Annabel turned he saw the tears in her eyes and the pink patches which had appeared on each of her cheeks, and his face fell. "Are you OK?"

"My foot hurts," she said. "But it's all right, I can walk."

"Come on, then."

She took one last look at the stone horse, then she hitched up the old coat and stood by Sebastian's side.

In silence, they set off together.

PART THREE
The Glass Gazebo

AT THE FOOT OF
THE MOUNTAIN

Annabel slept for a long time, swaddled in the lacy duvet on Janet's bed. In her dreams a yellow-eyed stone horse bucked and leapt in an irrational world. And when she awoke, the real world had changed.

The sky wasn't the hostile one under which she'd fled from Lucy. It wasn't the electric one which had witnessed the creation of the stone horse. Outside Janet's half-open window the sun was sailing confidently on a sea of cotton wool clouds. A breeze twitched the net curtains, bringing to Annabel's nostrils the smells of wet earth and steaming hay fields.

She sat up. She must get out there and see what Norman was up to. And she was hungry, too.

The rug by the bed tickled her bare soles. When she put her weight on them she gasped. The graze on her instep spread like a hastily drawn map towards her toes. But underneath it was only bruised. Despite her shivering, bedraggled, limping appearance last night, which had sent a hysterical Janet to the phone and taken the doctor away from his dinner table, nothing was seriously injured.

She sat on the edge of the bed, remembering how Sebastian had put his coat around her shoulders and responded to her mood. She thought about the openness with which he'd told her his feelings, and his suggestion about the gazebo. What was he doing at this moment? Pacing around under this bright sky, regretting it all?

Reality would have crept back to him by now, as it was creeping back to her. She reached for her dressing-gown. The optimism she'd felt when she'd woken to the sparkling morning faded. Was it really possible to make sculptures in the face of Janet and Frank's derision, Lucy's disbelief and Mr Lefevre's laughter? Or was she, as usual, dreaming?

It wasn't quite like a dream, though. It was more like being in someone else's life. She felt as if she'd been challenged to climb the sheer wall of a mountain and unfurl a flag on the summit. But she couldn't do it. The maker of the stone horse, whoever she was, would complete the climb, leaving anxious, pallid little Annabel forever at the foot of the mountain.

She got up and limped across the room to

the window. Everything outside looked brand new. Janet was inspecting the storm-ravaged garden in an elderly striped cotton dress and wellington boots. As she straightened up from the geranium bed she caught sight of Annabel at the window. She took off her gardening gloves and waved. "Darling, you're awake! Feeling better?"

"Yes, thanks!" called Annabel, waving back.

"Just let me get my wellies off, then!"

Maybe there were different kinds of dreams, thought Annabel. The dream she'd had about Sebastian, which was a fantasy with no chance of fulfilment, was one kind. Yesterday's dreamlike experience, during which she'd retreated from the real world and entered one which contained only herself and the stones, was another kind. But a dream you had about really wanting to *do* something – that kind of dream *could* come true, couldn't it?

Janet's slippers pattered up the stairs. She put a squelchy kiss on Annabel's cheek. "How's the foot?"

"It's OK, thanks."

Annabel was sitting in the corner of the wide windowsill. There wasn't much room, but Janet sat down in the other corner. "Are you sure?" she asked. Annabel could see grey smudges under her eyes.

"I'm sure, Janet. It's only a bruise."

151

Worried though she was, Janet couldn't resist some disapproval. "But what were you doing, messing about up there in the middle of a thunderstorm? You could have drowned, you know. Frank says that stream swells a lot after heavy rain, and runs fast."

"Not fast enough to drown me. Honestly, I was perfectly all right."

"Well, I just hope you were." She sounded unconvinced. "And what on earth was that boy doing there in the pouring rain too? I mean, what can you both have been doing?"

Annabel looked at the garden. "What do you think we were *doing*?"

"Well … nothing," said Janet discontentedly. "I just want to know what happened, that's all."

"We talked."

"But why did you go there in the first place?"

Annabel hesitated. Why *had* she gone there? Because she hadn't wanted to come home? Because the silver tunnel reminded her of Sebastian? Because she was a fool?

"I went there because it's a place I like to be, I suppose." Snapshots came into her mind. Sebastian crouching below her, searching her eyes, seeing the truth. The bleak, uncomprehending anxiety on his rain-splashed face. The tug-of-war she'd felt in her heart. "And Sebastian's a perfectly civilized person, you know."

152

Janet couldn't allow this. She wriggled her shoulders. "Well, *I* don't think he's very civilized. He behaved like a hooligan, stealing Frank's car—"

"Hardly *stealing*."

"Taking it without permission, then. And going off with that Lucy without telling anyone."

"I wish you wouldn't say 'That Lucy', as if she's a bad influence on me. You don't know her at all."

"Oh, come on. Everyone in Broughton knows how Miss Fast Forward behaves." She clutched the sleeve of Annabel's dressing-gown in sudden panic. "You won't tell her mother I said that, will you?"

Despite everything, Annabel smiled. "Janet..." she began.

But Janet was ready with one of her pseudo-questions, to which she always knew the answer herself. "And what about that rumpus in the garden on Sunday? Was that *civilized*?"

"What rumpus?"

"Don't deny it, Annabel. Lisa Turnbull looked quite put out."

"Laura," corrected Annabel automatically.

Her memory framed a clear picture of the buttercup field. Let Lucy deny it as much as she liked, Sebastian *had* encouraged Annabel to step over the wall. She'd followed him, and Lucy had stayed in the garden. He'd stood

153

there grinning, his midday shadow an inkblot on the grass, and taunted her. "Come and get it, then!" he'd said. She could hear his voice now, and see him waving the book.

Her heart flipped. Wait a minute. He hadn't spoken until she was *already in the field*. Could he possibly have wanted *Lucy* to chase him, but settled for Annabel when Lucy refused to play? Oh, no. *No.*

"Don't worry about Sebastian, sweetheart," Janet was saying. "He's going home after the holidays." She gave a long, deflating-tyre sigh. "You know, when he first arrived, I felt pretty hopeful. I thought it would be nice for him to get to know his father. And us, of course." She patted Annabel's hand. "But he's only been here a week and already he's caused all this trouble. Frank's so disappointed!"

In her heart Annabel knew that at last Sebastian had behaved properly. Janet wouldn't consider his gentlemanliness last night as sufficient excuse for his previous conduct, but he'd acted like the nice boy she'd always hoped he was. He'd treated her as if he *did* like her after all.

"Cheer up, chicken!" said Janet, recovering her smile. "I've got some news for you."

Annabel gazed at her, half in dread, half in anticipation. "What news?"

"Dad's coming to see us tomorrow!"

The words opened the door to a place

154

Annabel hadn't entered for a week.

"Oh…" She tried to rearrange her thoughts. "That's nice."

"I expect he'll take you out somewhere."

Annabel didn't reply.

"You're not worrying about Dad and Frank, are you, best beloved?"

Annabel still didn't reply.

"Old Frank's all right, you know," said Janet briskly. "Dad's known him a long time. And neither of them are the sort of person to make a fuss." She stood up, stretching. "I must get back to my borders. You can get your own breakfast, can't you?"

Annabel nodded.

"Don't brood on it, will you, darling?" Her voice was faintly aggrieved, as if she considered Annabel's concern unreasonable. "A woman needs a man, you know."

When she'd gone Annabel knelt up on the windowsill to get a better view across the hay-fields to Cairncross. She could see the ever-green thicket which bordered the Horwell road, and the lane where she'd leaned against the wall and thought about Sebastian. The house itself was lower down, though, and invisible.

A woman needs a man. But the books Janet was always quoting from preached feminine independence, and Janet considered herself free of the imaginary chains Dad had kept her

155

in. So why exchange Dad's chains for Frank's?

She put her forehead against the window pane. Beyond the garden the golden fields hovered like a mirage. Somewhere over there, behind that tangle of trees, Sebastian was asking Frank about the gazebo.

Her imagination leapt forward, to a day when the sun would be a little lower in the sky. A day in September. She saw Sebastian fold his legs into his aeroplane seat. She saw him accept a cup of coffee from the stewardess and sip it, the steam condensing on the tip of his nose. With his other hand, she saw him take out a photograph, dog-eared from much handling, and look at it with satisfaction.

Closing her eyes, she hugged the thought tightly. He was braving the sarcasm of a father he hardly knew for a girl he knew even less. And he wasn't trying to get something for himself, like the car. For some reason, he was doing this enormous, unselfish thing for no one but Annabel.

Dream on, Barbie-Brain, she told herself. The photograph will be of Lucy.

UNDER GLASS

Jed was familiar with the gazebo. He slipped through the half-open door and jumped up at the windows, wagging his tail. Sebastian pushed the door a few more centimetres. "Come on in, then. What are you waiting for?"

Annabel hesitated. After the steep climb to the gazebo, her injured foot was protesting more than she wanted Sebastian to know.

"Come *on*, will you?" he insisted, still holding the door. "It's perfectly safe."

The gazebo had so many sides it was almost circular. Each side was an arched window, and the roof was glass too. All the windows seemed to be gathered in at the top by a little dome decorated with carved leaves. Annabel went in and stood beside Sebastian in the centre of the floor, her weight on her good foot. With a sense of wonder she gazed through the glass at the unfolding view of Broughton in its valley, with the hills beyond.

She sat down clumsily on the iron bench which ran around the inside of the glass walls. Jed's nose nudged her knee. "Sebastian, this place is…"

"Amazing?"

She nodded slowly. After the events of the past week she felt she shouldn't be amazed at anything. But the gazebo truly *was* amazing.

"I told you," he said proudly. "Pretty good light, see?"

"Excellent," agreed Annabel, still nodding. She looked up. "It won't leak, will it?"

Sebastian sat down opposite her. He looked as if he was tempted to call her Barbie-Brain, but stopped himself. "Look at the floor, Annabel. It's completely dry."

It had rained every night for almost a week. Loud, clattering rain on her bedroom windows, waking her up then being so interesting to listen to that she couldn't go to sleep again.

She looked at the floor, and at Jed, who gazed back with brown velvet eyes. "Did your mother have a dog?" she asked Sebastian.

"How do I know? I told you, he never mentions her."

"She might have sat here, on this very bench," said Annabel. "With a dog just like Jed."

"Maybe." He looked doubtful. "Martha –

158

that's my aunt – says she liked it here. She thought it was peaceful."

"Well, she was right," said Annabel, smoothing Jed's ears. "I can't hear anything, except birdsong. Can you hear anything with these lovely long ears, Jed?"

Sebastian leaned forward, his elbows on his knees. His baseball cap – the white one he'd worn on the tennis court – hid the top half of his face. Knowing he couldn't see her, Annabel watched him run his tongue around his mouth between his lips and his teeth, preparing to speak.

"Martha says my mother loved horses," he said. "She ran a little riding school."

Annabel was surprised. "Here, at Cairn-cross?"

"Sure." He didn't look up. He clasped his hands very tightly. "I know, I know. There are no horses now. But the stable yard's still there, with the boxes the horses were kept in."

"Perhaps your father sold them when she … you know, when he lost her."

"I guess he did."

The subject seemed closed, but Sebastian hurried to speak again. "And that's not the only thing." The peak of his cap came up. Annabel saw his usual wide-awake expression, bordered with perplexity. "I was talking to the woman who runs the newspaper store a couple of days ago, and she was saying what a shame it was about my mother. You know, she was so young and pretty and all. I said – just to make conversation, I guess – that it was tough to die in a road accident, and she didn't seem to understand me. She kept shaking her head and talking about someone called Cassandra. It was Cassandra, she said."

"Who's Cassandra?" asked Annabel.

"I wish I knew, Annabel."

Annabel's heart felt squeezed. The frustrated joylessness in Sebastian's voice unnerved her. "Your father would know," she said.

"But how can I ask him? He's so weird about stuff like that. Don't you think he's weird?"

Annabel looked at the leaf-strewn floor. "He's difficult to get to know. He's a bit… er… brisk. But I think he must be OK, in his heart." She kicked some leaves with the side of her unbruised foot. "Look, I know this sounds stupid, but—"

"What?"

She didn't look at him. "It's just that he can't be so bad or Janet wouldn't want to marry him." Her neck was going pink. She swung her hair forward. "She divorced my dad before he bored her to death, she says, so she must like Frank better."

"You mean she thinks my dad *isn't* boring? Boy, what planet does she live on?"

160

Annabel had often wondered this herself. "Planet Janet, I suppose!"

She steadied her nerve and kept still, watching Sebastian's face. His nerve collapsed first. Uneasily, he slid his gaze away. "Did Janet tell you they've fixed the wedding for August twenty-ninth?"

She blinked. "No, she didn't. In Broughton Church?"

"I don't think so," he said gently. "It'll be a civil ceremony, in the banqueting suite of that fancy hotel. Your mom's divorced, so…"

"Oh, of course! I knew that."

Jed had gone outside to chase birds. His prey flew into a tree and the dog stood at the bottom, barking furiously. Annabel watched him, wondering if he would be coming to live with them when Janet and Frank were married. The thought of what Norman would make of such an arrangement almost made her smile.

"What day is it today?" asked Sebastian.

"Thursday."

"No, what's the date?"

She counted in her head. "August the sixth?"

"Three weeks and two days, then. I go back to the States on September fifth."

Goosebumps crept over Annabel, covering first her legs, then her arms, then the back of her neck. Every day, every hour, every minute she spent with Sebastian brought her nearer to losing him. To stepbrotherhood and then, a week later, to America. Hollowly, she said, "I hope your dad can afford the Swallowdale Hotel."

"Oh, sure he can. This redneck stuff's just an act, you know." He sat back against the window, straightening his legs. "That reminds me – what did your dad say about getting you some materials?"

She twisted round on the seat so that her hair hid her face. "I didn't ask him."

"Why not?" She heard his feet move among the leaves as he bent his legs again, and leaned forward.

"Well..." It was four days ago, but the thought of it still made her stomach hurt. "I watched for him coming all Sunday morning. In the end Janet told me to go out in the garden before I gave her a nervous breakdown."

"So did he come?"

"No." She had half-twisted back again, and was half-looking at him. "He phoned on Sunday afternoon to say he'd been held up, and couldn't get here after all. He said I could come down to London for a few days soon and he'll take me on the river, and shopping in Oxford Street. But..."

He gazed at her unhappily. "Well?"

"But I won't go."

"Why not?"

"I don't know. It was something about the way he spoke on the phone. It was just different." She returned his unhappy look. "*My* dad and I will never be the same together again, because of *your* dad. It was stupid of me to think we could be."

Sebastian frowned despondently. "You've told him about the horse, though, haven't you? And the gazebo?"

"No."

"But—"

"One day I will, but not yet. After the wedding, I think."

He didn't protest any more, but was obviously disappointed. He took off his cap and ran his hand over his head. Paintbrush-tips of dark hair stood up here and there, giving him the look of a much younger boy. His lower lip, she noticed for the first time, was slightly fuller than his upper one. His nose was straight like Frank's, and so were his eyebrows, but his face had a general curviness. The sun shone through the window behind him, turning the lobes of his ears pink.

In a rush Annabel realized that she was looking at him more closely than she'd ever looked at anyone. And as she looked, an idea planted itself in her brain. A wonderful, frightening idea. She took her next breath too quickly, and coughed.

"What's the matter?" asked Sebastian.

She had her hand over her mouth. She didn't move. She didn't say anything.

"Look, Annabel, I could use some coffee." Sighing, he put his cap on and stood up. "Let's go back to the house, OK?"

Still she didn't move. Impatient now, he turned away from her. Then he turned back. "What is it? Are you sick?"

"Sebastian…"

It wasn't a question, or an answer. She said the word slowly, like a foreign word she'd never pronounced before, clinging to the "n" at the end as if she couldn't bear to let it go.

Sebastian's muscles tensed. He sat down again. "What is it?"

"I've just had an idea. What if … what if…" She stopped, organized her thoughts, and began again. "What if I made a sculpture for Janet and Frank, for a wedding present? That would convince them I can do it, wouldn't it?"

Sebastian didn't speak.

"I mean, they're going to get married regardless of how we feel about it, aren't they? So we might as well be nice to them."

Sebastian still didn't speak. He was sitting very still, barely breathing, regarding her with a glimmering, watchful gaze. Annabel looked at the church tower in the valley, trying to control the storm-wave which had swirled over her. What was it? Fear? Desire? Embarrassment? How could you fear something you desired? And why be embarrassed about it?

She looked back at Sebastian. If only he didn't look so *beautiful*. If he was just ordinary, embarrassment wouldn't be an option. But it was his beauty which made her idea so irresistible.

She didn't say anything for a few moments. Then she swivelled round on the bench, her hands between her knees, and looked bravely under the peak of the baseball cap. "Don't you think it would be good if the present was from both of us?"

His face blanked out.

"What I mean is, if you'll let me..." She smiled widely suddenly. She couldn't help it. "I want to make a sculpture of *you*."

THE ONLY BOY IN THE BOY-FREE ZONE

Annabel fingered the cover of the book, not opening it. *Jane Eyre*, by Charlotte Brontë.

She decided to put it back on the shelf. She already had four books under her arm – three large, illustrated books on sculpture and a smaller one on watercolour technique. The library only let you have five, and she was tempted by a book about how to draw horses. A novel would have to wait until next time.

She put it back. Then, hesitating, she took it down again. She'd promised herself, after all. Recently the idea of reading a proper book had become, if not positively attractive, at least less repellent than it used to be. She pictured Laura Turnbull curled up on her duvet cover with the pink flying horses on it, scanning the crumpled pages of *The Dreamboat of Firewater Lake* with her lips parted and her marble-eyes bulging. She opened the book randomly.

The print was small and the words looked difficult. Astonishingly, the heroine was sometimes addressed as "Janet", though there was no Annabel or Lucy. Sebastian had once told the girls, only semi-joking, that their names belonged in an old book. She smiled to herself, wondering whether Sebastian, for all his showing off in front of Lucy, had actually read anything the Brontës had written.

"Annabel?"

She turned, slipping *Jane Eyre* between her other books, and was surprised to see Sean Turnbull leaning against the *H* to *M* section of the fiction shelves. His hair had grown since she last saw him. The forelock was falling into his eyes. She smiled. "Hello, Sean."

He smiled back. A very wary sort of smile. Annabel pretended to be looking at the *A* to *G* novels. "I thought you were on holiday, in Italy or somewhere."

"Greece. We got back yesterday. It was great. Incredibly hot."

She glanced at him. "I can see it was."

Under the sunburn his cheeks coloured. Annabel reflected that in his situation, hers would have too. It couldn't have been easy for him to approach her after what had happened on the tennis court that day. But, on the whole, she was glad he had.

Tomorrow it would be two weeks since he and Sebastian had squared up to each other. It was already two weeks since Annabel had first set eyes on the red and white baseball cap between the trees. And it was over a week since Lucy's fury had shattered the peace of that sunlit sitting room. Eventually, someone would have to break the spell Sebastian had cast on them all.

Sean looked at his watch. She noticed that the hairs on his forearm had been bleached even lighter than usual. "Look, I'm finished with these notes," he said, indicating the folder stuffed with papers in the crook of his elbow. "If you've got your books, shall we go for a coffee at Brown's?"

Annabel's surprise that he had spoken to her at all turned to amazement. She could feel herself, annoyingly, reddening. "All right, then." She dipped her head, swinging her hair forward. "Thanks. I'll just get these stamped."

At the desk, her blush disappeared at the same rate as her apprehension grew. Why had she accepted Sean's invitation? She didn't want to sit in Brown's with a boy she'd only liked because he'd been the only boy in the Boy-free Zone. She watched the assistant stamp her books, panic jerking her heart. She had to think of an excuse. Now, before they left the library.

"Sean…"

He was leaning against the wall outside. He straightened up when he saw her, pushing back his hair. "Ready?"

"Yes. Well, no. Look…"

"Your mum's not with you, is she?"

"No. She's gone off with Frank somewhere. But listen, I—"

"I hear they're getting married," he said cheerfully, and set off along the High Street. Annabel had to follow. "Laura told me, needless to say. Not much of a surprise, I suppose!"

Annabel said nothing. She couldn't possibly admit that it *had* been a surprise to her. Sean already thought she was stupid enough.

"Look," he said, quickening his pace. "The window table's free. If we shift a bit we'll get it."

Defeated, Annabel trailed after him, watching his back view as it dodged between the passers-by. His shoulders *did* slope, that was certain. And he was skinny in a way that Sebastian wasn't. His gold-red hair looked nice in the sunshine, though. She remembered how it had flapped like that when he'd danced in her set at the Scouts' Barn Dance, and how excitement had fizzed inside her as she waited for him to catch her hand.

What was the matter with her? Didn't she have anything better to do than look at boys? Was she turning into the sex maniac Janet was always saying "That Lucy" was? Or was it just that for the first time she was looking at boys not just as boys, but as *people*?

Perhaps, she thought as she slid into the seat by the window, it was only after you'd got over being impressed by someone's physical appearance that you could look at the person behind it. Her experiences with Sebastian in the gazebo had shown her that.

He had bought the clay for the secret sculpture himself, and carried it up to the gazebo in a wheelbarrow while his father was at work. For two days now, Annabel had worked on the preliminary drawings. The more drawings she did, the stronger Sebastian's likeness became. And the more she looked at him, the better she knew him.

Positioned in the very centre of the gazebo, he seemed to soak up the light and shower it all around him. It bounced off every hair, every muscle, every contour of his face and neck. It slid over his features, reappearing in different forms in his eyes, or the glistening of his teeth, or reflecting off his fingernails when he put his hand up to his face.

Mr Lefevre sometimes talked about great painters whose whole lives were devoted to the pursuit of light, as they tried to find ways of putting it on canvas. Light is the basis of painting, he said. It captures the beauty of the presence of things. Well, it was the basis of sculpture too, it seemed to Annabel. It captured the beauty of the presence of Sebastian. As he sat there, impatient, bored, asking her every few minutes if she'd finished yet, the light illuminated his outer surfaces and angles and textures. But somehow, it showed up what was on the inside, too.

"Ice-cream, or just coffee?" asked Sean, arranging his notes in a pile.

"Oh, coffee," said Annabel vaguely. Her digestive juices were unmoved by the bright pictures on the menu card. She didn't even want coffee, really.

Sean ordered two coffees and a Rum 'n' Raisin Surprise. Annabel watched the boy in the paper hat scraping up pinky-beige scoops and arranging them in a tall glass. He didn't catch her eye, though. With a stab of understanding she realized why. Usually she was with Lucy. Today she was with a boy.

She looked at Sean. He had freckles, but his freckles weren't like the ice-cream boy's freckles. They were better behaved, or something. They were vital to the way he looked, so that if you took them away he wouldn't be Sean, but they didn't make him look bad. They just *were* him.

"What have you been doing for the past two weeks, then?" he asked pleasantly. "Not playing tennis, I hope!"

It was brave of him to mention it. "No, not playing tennis," she said bashfully. "I've got no talent for that. But I've discovered I can do something else." She lifted *Jane Eyre*, revealing

171

the pile of art books. "You know I like art, don't you?"

"Er..."

"Well, I've recently discovered how interesting sculpture is."

His attention sharpened.

"Look at these books." She pushed them towards him, opening the top one. "Aren't these things beautiful? I want to make things like these. No, better than these."

He looked down at the pictures. "How?" he asked. "I mean, how can *you* do sculpture? Don't you need huge blocks of stone, or a blow-torch, or something?"

She smiled. It was strange, to be more knowledgeable about something than a boy whose mother boasted of his Oxford aspirations. "Well, there are lots of different kinds of sculpture, you know. I made a horse from loose stones, like the drystone walls my grandad used to build."

He didn't speak. His dappled eyes narrowed slightly, inviting her to go on.

"It was a horse lying on its side, with its head down," she told him. "You couldn't make a standing-up horse from dry stones, of course. But just because it wasn't carved from a block of marble, or cast in bronze, that doesn't mean it wasn't a sculpture."

Their order came. Annabel looked doubtfully at the frothy liquid, knowing she would spill it when she tried to lift the shallow cup. She resolved to wait until Sean lifted his and copy what he did.

He took a mouthful of ice-cream, digging around the edge of the glass, licking the spoon. It wasn't too disgusting to watch, though. And she was flattered by his unforced interest in what she was saying. "So sculpture can be made of anything, then?" he said.

"Pretty well." She spun the book round and searched its pages. "Here, look. This picture shows a sculpture made of scrap metal, and this one's like a fountain, with water running all over it. And this one's made of clay. Lots of sculptors work in clay. You can coat it with latex, which dries to make a mould, which you fill with some quick-setting material."

"Like the plaster figures I used to make for Laura? Of cartoon characters and so on?"

"Exactly." She closed the book. "And you can make sculptures out of papier-mâché, or wire mesh, or sheet metal, or wood, or cardboard. People even sculpt from ice, and snow, and wet sand. I'm going to have a go at all of them. In fact, I've already started to make something out of clay."

This wasn't strictly true. The clay was still in its polythene bag. But Annabel had freed herself from the fear of doing something new by preparing properly, as Mr Lefevre always said. She'd revised Dad's lessons about squaring up and measuring and getting the proportions right. She'd copied pictures and instructions in books, sketching, experimenting and destroying, and trying again.

She and Sebastian had decided on a pose with his head turned, showing the tendons of the neck. He wouldn't be able to hold the position for long, but she had her drawings, and the photographs she'd taken with his expensive camera. With the greenhouse heat of the gazebo beating down on her scalp, she'd planned the sculpture to be as accurately life-size as she could make it. It had to be right. It had to be more than the dead representation of a living person. She didn't know how to do it, but she had to give it a life-force.

Sean was smiling. She noticed that his front teeth crossed each other a little and he had a minuscule dimple just to the left of his mouth. He picked up his coffee without spilling any, but Annabel was so interested in looking at him that she forgot to watch how he did it. "Does your mum let you do all this on her kitchen table?" he asked.

"Well, no." She paused. "I've managed to get a – sort of a studio, I suppose."

"A *studio*? Annabel…"

She mined deep reserves of courage. "It was Sebastian's idea. He got his father to let me work in the gazebo – a sort of glasshouse – at Cairncross. He says that if Frank's going to be

174

my stepfather he'd better get used to having me around."

Sean was watching her from under his hair. "You're incredible," he said.

"Incredibly daft, you mean?" She thrust her thumb confidently through the handle of her coffee cup. It tilted. The coffee slopped in the saucer.

"No, incredibly enterprising. I always thought…" He looked out of the window.

Annabel rescued him. "I'm surprised at myself, too," she confessed. "Miss Fitzwilliam – that's our Headteacher – told me last term that my brain's as much use as a suitcase with no lid. Everything you put in just falls out again. But maybe I've changed, or something."

Sean looked like someone who can't find anywhere to park their dead chewing gum. Embarrassed, unwilling to break any rules, but desperate. "It sounds like Sebastian House-man's changed too."

"No, I don't think he has."

Annabel pictured the intensity of Sean's fury that day on the tennis court, and wondered if he would hate Sebastian for ever, whatever happened. Then another picture came into her mind, of someone else's hatred.

She picked up her cup. "Have you seen Lucy?"

"Laura saw her last night, at the paper shop." He said this cautiously, as if he expected her to be offended. "She thought she seemed a bit grumpy. You know, out of sorts."

"Oh. Perhaps she's ill. Or perhaps…"

Sean looked thoughtful, but didn't prompt her.

"Perhaps we've been spending too much time together." This didn't occur to her until the instant she said it. She put the cup down again without drinking any coffee. "We could do with a little while away from each other, I think."

Sean was tactful enough to see that she was unwilling to explain. He swirled the dregs of his coffee around the bottom of the cup. "Anything the matter with your coffee?"

Annabel looked sheepish.

"You should have the courage of your convictions," he said, without scorn. "You prefer Apple Fizz, don't you? I'll get you one."

She watched him walk to the counter, his fingers closing round the wallet in the back pocket of his trousers. And as she watched she became aware that a secret, furtive idea was struggling out of darkness. Despite what Sean had just said to her, she *did* have the courage of her convictions.

The stone horse had shown her something mysterious, which both thrilled and disconcerted her. It had shown her that sculpture could contain the feelings of the person who made it. But now, suddenly, she understood that it could also contain the feelings of the person who was *in* it.

Under the glass roof of the gazebo, her desire to make a sculpture of Sebastian's head and shoulders had taken root and grown strong. And the more time she spent with him – what would Lucy say, if she knew? – the more she understood *his* feelings, too. The puzzle had begun to solve itself.

Sebastian was mixed up. He resented being summoned to England just as deeply as he resented being banished to America. As she'd sat there drawing him he'd told Annabel about all the possessions and privileges he had at home. But he'd talked mostly about Frank. He wanted his father to love him as his aunt and uncle did. But Frank didn't know this, and treated him like a stranger.

She looked out at the busy Saturday street, and something momentous struck her. If sculpture could contain feelings, could it also enable – perhaps even *force* – the people who looked at it to have feelings, too? Sebastian carried round his quest for his father's approval like excess baggage with no check-in point. Yet Frank's eyes were closed to it. Could it be her hands, literally, which held the power to open them?

THE GOO-GOO MAN

Annabel's Maid of Honour dress was pale
blue, with a flounced skirt, puffed sleeves and
a sweetheart neckline. It wasn't flattering.
Janet's full-length mirror reflected a little girl
in an overstarched party frock.

"Beautiful, darling! A Dresden shepherdess!" Janet scraped Annabel's hair into a top-
knot, stabbing her scalp with the pins, and
crowned it with a wreath of imitation flowers.
"We're going to have pink roses – real ones, of
course – on the day. I wanted white, but Frank
says I can't have York roses because I'm not a
native of Yorkshire. And I certainly can't have
red Lancaster ones!"

Annabel's dismay increased. She didn't
want to be a Dresden shepherdess with pink
roses round her head. She didn't want to spend
a long August day in a tight sash and three
petticoats. In fact, she didn't want to go to

the wedding at all.

The prospect of watching Sebastian become her stepbrother filled her with dread. He was still the boy whose power to thrill her had shaken her so violently. He was still the cause of the most serious quarrel she and Lucy had ever had. And the passion she'd felt while the thunder broke over the silver tunnel had been for no one but him. Despite the friendship which he had unexpectedly shown her, the slightest reminder of the intensity of that feeling still made her palms sweat.

It only took a split-second to fall in love, it seemed. But it took years to learn how to deal with it.

"Why can't I just have something ordinary, which I can wear again after the wedding?" she asked.

"Because this wedding isn't going to be *ordinary*," said Janet, pulling viciously at Annabel's sash. "I had an ordinary wedding when I married your father – that terrible navy suit! – and this time I'm having proper dresses." She stood back. "Is that too tight, baby? It has to be fairly tight, to give you a figure. Can you breathe?"

"No," said Annabel, ducking out of the way. "I'll do it myself. I'm not a child, though I look like one in this frock."

"But baby, it's lovely!"

Annabel re-tied the bow. "Do I *have* to wear

179

it?" she asked, searching her mother's reflected face for the smallest sign of doubt.

"Of course you do," said Janet. She bent down to fluff out the flounce. "It's paid for."

Annabel sighed. "What would your student friends say if they saw it? Everything they wear looks like it came from the Oxfam shop. The sale rail at the Oxfam shop, in fact."

"Don't be so catty. And anyway, they *will* see it," said Janet, straightening up. "Now, take it off and let's see about shortening that petticoat."

Annabel was surprised. "They're coming to the wedding?"

"I've invited quite a crowd," said Janet briskly. She unzipped the back of the dress. "I told you, it's going to be a very special day for Frank and me."

You don't know how special, thought Annabel, struggling out of the puffed sleeves. The thought of Janet gaping at Sebastian's sculpted head emboldened her. Before she could change her mind she voiced a question she'd been longing to ask. "Is that why Frank got Sebastian over here? Because he wanted him to come to the wedding? Sebastian says he sent him a *fax*, of all things. It was more of a command than an invitation."

Janet hung up the crumpled dress, smoothing the material like a theatrical dresser. She didn't look at Annabel. "Actually, if you want

180

the truth, it was my idea."

"The fax?" said Annabel faintly.

"No, of course not. Getting him over here, as you so charmingly put it."

Annabel slipped her blue and white checked top over her shoulders and began to do up the buttons. "You wanted him to get to know us so that he'd accept the bombshell when you and Frank dropped it, didn't you?"

The words were Sebastian's. Janet's mouth opened and shut, but she didn't speak. She teased out the gathered skirt of the dress. Annabel could tell by her distracted, rapidly moving eyes that she was thinking fast.

She seized the advantage. "And Dad knew you were about to announce it, so he cleared off to London at the crucial moment. Didn't he?"

"Annabel, *please*." Janet left the dress alone. She sat down with a small thud on the tapestry chair beside the bed. "Please don't try to – oh, I don't know – to make something up which isn't there."

"What do you mean?"

"About Dad, darling." Janet's voice was a bit higher than usual. "You're not a child, as you're always saying. And you've certainly shown some maturity over this wedding business. But you've got to grow up about Dad, too."

"What?" She still didn't understand.

"Sit down, sweetheart."

Annabel sat down on the bed, which was covered with taffeta underskirts and the tissue paper they'd come in. Janet pushed them aside and sat beside her.

"Do you think Dad's living alone in London, baby?"

Annabel didn't think anything. She was incapable of thought.

"Well, he isn't. He's living with this person who offered him the partnership. She's a widow, and the company was her husband's. Dad met her last year at a Builders' Federation Conference in Birmingham. He's going to be her partner in more ways than one, if you see what I mean. Her name's Stephanie."

Stephanie. Annabel heard the word but couldn't register its meaning.

"When they're settled he plans to invite you to meet her. But one wedding's enough to deal with at once, he said, and I think he's right." She put her arm around Annabel's shoulders. "We always try to do what's best for you, darling, though you don't always see it like that."

Annabel thought about pushing her away and bursting into tears. Or fainting, like she'd done when Frank had produced the engagement ring. But those tactics seemed unproductive now.

"I'm incredibly stupid," she said. "I'm the most incredibly stupid person in the whole incredibly stupid world."

Janet chuckled throatily. "No, you're not. You're actually getting more sensible. You're learning to think about other people as well as yourself. In a family, you know, everyone's happiness depends on everyone else's."

The truth of this crashed down on Annabel with some force. "What's she like, this Stephanie? Have you met her?"

"Oh, no. Dad only ever sees her in London. Imagine how the tongues would start wagging if he brought her here!"

Annabel thought about Broughton's wagging tongues, which had been the reason Frank hadn't talked about his wife or his son. And it had been to avoid small town gossip that he and Janet had sat on their own secret for so long. Mrs Evans had a lot to answer for. And so did her apprentice, Laura Turnbull.

The doorbell rang. Janet and Annabel looked blankly at each other. "Finish dressing, darling," said Janet, "and I'll go and see who it is."

Her backless sandals clicked down the stairs. Annabel heard the creak of the front door. "My goodness!" exclaimed Janet. "Hello, stranger!"

"Hello, Mrs Bairstow," said a very well-known voice.

Lucy, at last.

Annabel pulled her skirt on and tore the pins

from her hair. Two weeks had passed since the day Annabel had come to think of as the Horse Day, though it might just as well be called the Lucy Day. Or even, like most of the days in the past three weeks, the Sebastian Day. Two weeks of silence from Lucy and silence from Annabel, broken by Janet's fatuous greeting.

Lucy was waiting in the hall wearing her best jeans and an expression poised between defiance and apology. Annabel recognized it from the many times Miss Fitzwilliam had ordered Lucy to wipe it off her face.

"Hello," she said, with the same shyness as she'd felt when she'd greeted Sean in the library. To be shy with *Lucy* was ridiculous, though.

"Hello yourself."

Annabel knew that, just like Dad, Lucy wasn't standing in exactly the same place beside her as she always had done, and never would again. But when Lucy spat on her hand she understood, and spat on her own.

"The Goo-Goo Man's goo-goo-goo-gone!" they said in unison, and slapped their palms together.

"We haven't done that since primary school," said Lucy when they'd stopped laughing. "I'm amazed we can still remember it!"

Annabel led the way into the kitchen, where Janet had left a jam-smeared plate on the table and gone outside. "We do the Goo-Goo Man and Janet eats doughnuts," she said. "Some things don't change."

"And some things do," said Lucy.

She was still Annabel's gypsy, on loan from her ancestral caravan. As Annabel looked at her a feeling came to her which she couldn't explain. Something to do with everyone's happiness depending on everyone else's. "Talk about midsummer madness!" she said, opening the fridge door and ducking behind it. "We must have been crazy, to get so worked up over ... er... Do you want a drink?"

Lucy sat down at the table and locked her feet round the legs of the chair. "What have you got?"

"Fizzy water, un-fizzy water or milk. Janet's on one of her health kicks."

Lucy giggled. "Doughnuts and all?"

"Of course. Let's have some milk with chocolate powder in it." She found the tin and two glasses, and poured the milk. "We used to drink this when we were little. Do you remember?"

"With those straws that went round and round," said Lucy happily.

They sipped the chocolate milk. The taste was instantly memorable. "Isn't it *sweet*!" exclaimed Annabel. "Why didn't our baby teeth go rotten?"

Lucy wrinkled her nose. "I'm not even sure I like it." She put down her glass, then picked it up again. "But I'll drink it, because you made it for me." She sipped again, without grimacing this time. "You're a good friend, Annabel. Better than I deserve."

Annabel was bewildered. Lucy didn't deserve *her*? She'd spent the last ten years trying to be like Lucy – clever, spirited, "a natural leader", as some besotted teacher had once written on her report. "Don't be silly," she said.

"No, you were really good about – you know, about Sebastian," said Lucy.

There was a pause. Neither of them hurried to drink any more chocolate milk. Annabel realized dimly that it wasn't its oversweet taste which discouraged them, but its connection with their childhood world. Neither she nor Lucy wanted to be reminded that the quarrel over Sebastian stood like a wall at the end of it.

"I didn't go out with him, you know, Luce," she said.

Lucy's eyelids drooped. "Of course you didn't."

"I *didn't*."

"Oh, sure," said Lucy, more doubtfully than sarcastically. "Like Sebastian didn't want to win that tennis match, I suppose?"

"Come on, don't start getting worked up again. I didn't see him because I couldn't face him."

"Why not?"

Annabel tried to put her thoughts into the right order. "I was confused. He made me feel – I don't know, like nobody had ever looked at me or touched me before. It was like discovering treasure, or something. And I even thought at first that he might like *me*. I had some stupid fantasy about giving him a picture of me to take home in his wallet."

Lucy's hand went to her mouth. "Next to his heart?"

"I suppose so."

"You're a romantic moron, Annabel."

Annabel smiled. She knew she was, but she didn't mind. And the Maid of Honour dress proved that she wasn't the only romantic moron in the world. "Anyway, when he behaved so badly, I just didn't know what to do with my feelings about him. Do you understand?"

"I think so."

"I felt awful," remembered Annabel. She looked at the table, fingering the edge of her glass. "I mean, it would have been all right if I could have just said to myself, OK, forget him, he isn't the nice boy you hoped for. But..." She raised her head, not caring if Lucy saw her eyes reddening. "I avoided him all week just like I told you. But I couldn't forget him – it was like he'd taken over my brain, so that I couldn't think about anything else. Oh, Lucy, I wanted him to like *me*, not *you*. I've behaved so stupidly, I'll still be blushing in fifty years' time."

"Even in the dark, in bed, when no one can see you?"

Annabel nodded. "Embarrassment factor one hundred per cent."

Lucy took hold of her glass but didn't pick it up. Annabel noticed that her hand was trembling. "*My* embarrassment factor must be two hundred per cent, then." Her face took on a desperate, confessional look. "In Haworth that day, in the car, I tried to get Sebastian to kiss me. I practically climbed into his lap. But he pushed me away as if I was repulsive to him. He said something about the teams not being equally matched, and that he'd acted like a jerk. I didn't understand what he meant. He apologized, but I was so upset I was nearly crying all the way back, and looked out of the window the whole time so he wouldn't see. It was the worst thing that's ever happened to me."

Annabel put out her hand across the table and grasped Lucy's fingers. Lucy grasped back, sniffing unhappily. "I fancied him like anything. And you have to admit he seemed to fancy me. But when he pushed me away like that ... oh, how can girls be so *dumb*?"

"We're not dumb," said Annabel. Lucy looked at her, impressed by the fervour in her

188

voice. "We're *not*. It's true, we thought that Sebastian would rescue us from the Boy-free Zone, but who can blame us? We're just ordinary girls who'd like to meet ordinary boys. That's not dumb, that's normal. When the most beautiful boy in the world turned up, what were we supposed to do – ignore him?"

"Do you think he's beautiful?" asked Lucy solemnly.

"Yes, of course."

"So do I. Boring, aren't we?"

"No, we're not boring, we're *normal*." Annabel got up and began to pace up and down the kitchen, though there wasn't much space to do it in. But she felt too agitated to sit still.

Lucy considered. "It wasn't just that he's beautiful, though. It was the way he was making up to me, in Houseman's yard. Did you see it?"

"Of course I did. And how do you think it made me feel?

"Poor old Barbie-Brain," said Lucy. Her eyes began to glitter. "I knew I should feel sorry for you, but I didn't. I was really glad when you refused to come. What a bitch!"

"Lucy, listen." Annabel stopped pacing and gripped the back of a chair. "You're not a bitch, and I'm not a – a Barbie doll. Sebastian made us *think* we are, but we're not. And do you know what the craziest thing of all is?"

189

"What?"

Annabel pulled the chair out and sat on it. She leaned towards Lucy, her hair swinging over her face. She flicked it impatiently behind her ears. "I know Sebastian much better now. In these last two weeks I've made friends with him. And he's turned out to be much nicer than we thought."

"Are you joking?" Lucy's eyes were very bright now, expectant and disbelieving. "How can he suddenly change? Has his Fairy Godmother waved a magic wand over him?"

"He hasn't changed." It was exactly what she'd told Sean. "He's still rude to people, and he still shows off. But now I can understand *why* he does those things, and forgive him because of what's *inside*, not because of the way he looks."

Lucy's eyes opened wide. She looked ready to laugh.

"I'm serious," said Annabel patiently. "It's hard to explain, but Sebastian's kind of *angry*. He's got this rage inside him, which has been building up for years. Against his father, really. But he took it out on innocent bystanders like us."

"So you've been seeing him over the last two weeks, then, have you?"

Annabel smiled. "Not *seeing* him, like a boyfriend. Anyway, he can't really be a boyfriend now, since he's going to be my brother." She looked at Lucy quickly. "You heard about that, did you?"

"I live in Broughton, don't I?"

"Well, all right." She collected her nerve. "Obviously, I've got to start treating him differently. I mean, he treats *me* differently."

"Like Sean treats Laura, you mean?"

This suggestion was so misguided Annabel felt a shock-wave pass through her body. "No!" she gasped. "Not at all. He just seems to see me as – as an equal."

"Oh, great. Hansel and Gretel. And who's the witch? No, don't tell me."

Annabel didn't care if Lucy teased her. Lucy had lost her powers of manipulation at exactly the same moment that Sebastian had surrendered his father's old waterproof coat. "Honestly, Luce. He's just like everyone else. He wants to be loved. More than anything, he wants his father to love him."

"Doesn't his father love him?"

"If your father sent you away to a foreign country and hardly took any notice of you for seventeen years, you'd wonder if he loved you, wouldn't you?"

Lucy nodded thoughtfully. "If Frank Houseman doesn't love Sebastian, though ... does that mean he doesn't love Janet either?"

"Lucy!" Annabel blinked. Lucy had hit on something she hadn't considered. Frank *did* love Janet, obviously. Could that single fact lie

191

at the bottom of Sebastian's tall pile of grievances against his father? "Oh, poor Sebastian!"

"Poor Sebastian indeed," said Lucy with feeling. "I'm sorry, Annabel, but I couldn't cope with having Janet as a stepmother, even if I lived thousands of miles away from her." She gave Annabel a mock-conspiratorial look, lowering her voice. "I think she's only marrying Frank Houseman for the chance of some trips to America. She's doing it for the *doughnuts*."

Annabel stood up, pulling Lucy with her. "Let's go upstairs and I'll show you the disgusting dress she's insisting I wear." She put her hands on Lucy's shoulders and propelled her out of the room. "And while we're up there I'll tell you all about my dad's girlfriend."

"*What?*"

"Sshh!" Annabel could see Janet through the window, coming towards the house. "Go on, the dress is in Janet's bedroom." She shut the kitchen door behind them. "And when you've finished being sick all over it, let's go and buy some proper drinks, as sticky and unhealthy as possible, and put them in the fridge, and see how long Janet lasts before she helps herself to one."

"Ten minutes, I give her," laughed Lucy.

"Five, maximum," said Annabel, and led the way upstairs.

IF MY HEART WERE A HORSE

At half-past three on the day of the wedding Annabel sat down in the rocking chair, washed up like a sea creature on an unfamiliar shore, gasping for normality. The excitement with which she'd worked on the sculpture had been replaced by a deep, numbing, questioning anxiety.

What if everything went wrong?

What if, despite the meticulous secrecy she and Sebastian had maintained, Janet and Frank already knew about the sculpture, and would have to pretend to be surprised? What if they didn't even recognize the head as Sebastian's? What if they *laughed*?

She looked across the room to where Sebastian stood. Once the day's events had swung unstoppably into action, the way she looked at him would be changed for ever. But for now, she looked at him like she always had. And he looked like he always did. Neat and clean and polished, like a brand new box of paints.

Gripping the arms of the chair, she plopped her satin pumps on to the floor and pushed herself to her feet. "I've changed my mind," she told Sebastian. "Let's not do it."

"Don't be ridiculous, Annabel."

She felt very hot. The sash of the blue dress cut her around the middle. Nausea rose, filling her mouth with saliva. "I *am* ridiculous. And I'm going to be sick."

"What's the problem?"

"I don't think I'm brave enough."

His wide eyes widened. "Are you crazy?"

The sitting room door opened and Frank came in, unrecognizably smart in a dark suit. Sebastian's only remotely formal garment was the white shirt he'd worn when he'd driven Lucy away in his father's car, and he wore it now, with a hired suit, a serious tie and new-looking black shoes.

Frank looked very nervous. "She'll be down in a minute," he said to no one. He stood in front of the fireplace, raising and lowering his heels. "Oh 'eck," he muttered. "Blasted wedding." He raised and lowered his heels again, said "Oh 'eck" again, and looked dolefully at the hearthrug.

"Well, she'd better hurry," said Sebastian, consulting his watch. "The car's coming in fifteen minutes, and we haven't given you

194

our present yet."

Frank's eyebrows bristled above his dark eyes, which weren't round like Sebastian's, but elliptical, like little boiled sweets. He nodded at the box which Sebastian had left in the middle of the sofa. "What's in it? Gold bullion?" This was one of his almost-jokes, which were the nearest thing to humour Annabel ever heard from him. He regarded her gravely. "Good job the wagon's got four-wheel drive, that's all I can say."

Sebastian sat down in the rocking chair Annabel had left. "Where's Janet?" he asked restlessly. "Shouldn't she be here by now?"

She was in the doorway. Poured into a cream lace dress like a jelly into a mould, with a tiny veiled pillbox hat on her pinned-up hair. Annabel had witnessed many previews of this moment, but Sebastian and Frank stared.

"Darlings!" said Janet, throwing out her arms like a film starlet. "I'm ready!"

Taking Janet's hand, Frank steered her to the centre of the room, took a pace backwards and gazed at her. "You look terrific. Bloody amazing."

It was the truth. Annabel had worried that Janet's longing for "proper dresses" would obliterate all possibility of good taste. The Maid of Honour dress hadn't done much to shake this worry off, but when Janet had come home from the dressmaker full of childlike excitement, and shown Annabel the exquisite lace and the discreet hat, she'd known all would be well.

Frank brushed Janet's cheek with his moustache. Tears suddenly threatened Annabel's fragile composure. She couldn't look at Sebastian.

"Is the car here?" asked Janet, her eyes like blue china saucers. "Where are my flowers?"

"We can't go yet," said Frank. He jerked his head towards the window, where Sebastian sat in the rocking chair and Annabel stood behind it, holding on to its back rods for support. "These two want to give us this famous present they've been so cagey about."

"Oh, yes!" Janet spun round. She caught sight of the box between the sofa cushions. "Is this it? Can I open it?"

"Go right ahead," said Sebastian. Annabel sensed his body stiffen. If my heart were a horse, she thought, it would be trotting.

Janet took the lid off the box. "Straw!" she exclaimed.

"Good grief," said Frank. "Don't tell me it's something breakable." Curiosity getting the better of him, he peered into the box. Janet parted the straw, and gasped.

"Pull the sides of the box down," instructed Sebastian. Annabel didn't look at him, but she heard the chair creak as he moved, and his uneven breathing. "It comes apart. I made it especially."

Frank sat down on the sofa. He tugged gently at one side of the box. Janet sat on the other side and extracted more straw. Neither of them spoke. The room was so quiet that Annabel could hear the ticking of the clock in the hall. If my heart were a horse, she thought, it would be cantering.

The head came out of the box like a swimmer rising from the sea, its left profile appearing first. When Frank saw, or suspected, what it was, he tore at the other three sides of the box with greater force. "Christ, Janet," he muttered, not noticing what he was saying. The back, and the right side, and then at last the full face appeared. Janet put both her hands over her mouth. Her eyes, bright with excitement, brightened more.

"My God, it's Sebastian," she breathed. "Frank, look – it's Sebastian."

Slowly, during the bright mornings and angry middays, and shorter and shorter afternoons of August, Sebastian's likeness had grown out of the clay. Bowed over her workbench, weeping occasionally with exhaustion or frustration, Annabel had concentrated so hard that the days blurred into each other. She could no longer remember how many had passed since she met Sebastian, or were left before the wedding. And in that strange glass studio, where sunshine and clouds chased each other across the roof and raindrops spattered the windows with a solid, gravelly sound, the sculpture had come, at last, to life.

Now that Janet and Frank had actually seen it Annabel felt calmer. She released the rods of the chair, hiding her damp hands between the gathers in her skirt. Sebastian, alerted by the rustle of the material, sought her right hand with his left. His fingers closed around hers. His hand was damp, too.

"Sure, it's my *head*," he explained to Janet, who was gazing in awe from his face to the sculpture and back again. "But it's Annabel's *hands*, because she made it. The whole thing was her idea."

"We did it together," insisted Annabel.

Sebastian was watching his father. "It's not bad for a first try, is it, Dad? Don't you think Annabel has a great talent?"

Frank hadn't moved. He sat beside the wrecked box, brushing the remaining fronds of straw from the sculpture. He touched the forehead and nose and cheeks tenderly. Annabel wondered in a panic if he was going to burst into tears. If my heart were a horse, she thought, it would be galloping.

"Frank?" Janet couldn't wait any longer. "Isn't Annabel clever? Aren't you proud of her? And isn't it a *fabulous* present?"

Frank wasn't listening. He was looking across the room to the window bay, where the afternoon sun shone on the nape of Annabel's neck, exposed by her upswept hair. A long beam slanted between the curtains, catching Sebastian's head a glancing blow and scattering into invisibility.

"Sebastian's so like his mother," croaked Frank. He cleared his throat. "When I saw the head in the box, for a minute I thought—" He took a handkerchief out of his breast pocket and wiped his forehead and fingers. "I thought she'd come back to me."

Sebastian let go of Annabel's hand. He leaned forward. His face wore an attentive, determined look, as if he'd been given an opportunity he wasn't prepared to lose. "She has, Dad. She's right here in the sculpture. She's in *me*."

He got up and crossed the room, and sat on the arm of the chair beside the sofa. Frank looked at him with eyes as dark and dull as Broughton's slate roofs.

"I thought you'd forgotten all about me," he said gruffly. "But Janet wanted you over here for the wedding. And now you're almost grown up, you look so like Nancy. That night she went out to the horses, she was only a couple of years older than you. A week past twenty, she was."

The sound of horses' hooves echoed in Annabel's head. She pressed her feet into the floor, tensing the muscles of her legs, waiting and wondering.

"Which night? Which horses?" asked Sebastian, with round eyes. "What happened?"

Janet put her arm protectively around the sculpture's shoulders. Frank's fingers were spread on the crown of its head. He put his other hand on Sebastian's real shoulder.

"Tell him, Frank," said Janet.

Slowly, Frank let go of Sebastian's shoulder and leaned his elbows on his knees, locking his fingers, looking at the floor. "Well, we kept horses at Cairncross in those days. One night Nancy went out to check 'em like she always did. One of the mares – Cassandra, its name was – went crazy when she went into its box. Nancy was pinned against the back wall. She didn't have a chance. The horse kicked her in the head and trampled on her, and she died in hospital two hours later. By that time I'd already shot the horse."

Annabel's leg muscles no longer wanted to hold her up. She sat down in the rocking chair, astonishment running over her like seawater over a sandcastle, filling every crevice of her body, sucking her down with it as it retreated. In her mind's eye, she could see the horse lying on the ground with its head stretched out as if asleep, or dead. The horse made of stones. And from some secret recess of her brain sprang a picture of Miss Fitzwilliam writing "Cassandra" on the blackboard. In ancient Greek mythology, she was saying, Cassandra was a prophetess. She had the power to foretell future events, but no one would believe her.

Sebastian swallowed and blinked. He couldn't speak. He made some sort of grunt.

"That was a terrible night, Sebastian," said Janet softly. "Your father blamed himself, but it wasn't his fault, or anybody's. Nancy was just in the wrong place at the wrong time."

"I usually went out to the stables with her," said Frank, still looking at the floor. "But it was proper damp that night, and frosty. I had a nasty cold, so she said she'd go alone." He paused, sighing a little. "And I let her."

Sebastian looked at him, then at Janet, then back at his father again, hopeful of more information.

"Even if he'd been there he couldn't have done anything, Sebastian," explained Janet. "It happened in a flash, like these things always do. If Frank had tried to restrain the horse he might have been killed too."

"I don't keep horses any more," said Frank, his voice thickening. "I never will again. May God forgive me, but I just couldn't stand to be reminded of her, by the horses or by you, Sebastian."

The dull look had gone from his eyes. They were agitated by the memories he'd disturbed. He looked at Sebastian, trying to control his expression, twitching his eyebrows. Annabel

201

was reminded of how he'd looked when he'd produced Janet's ring from his jacket pocket. "That's why I sent you away, you see," he said. "I thought I'd be able to forget what she looked like. But when I saw you at the airport, I – well, I just didn't know what to do."

"For God's sake, Dad!" Sebastian exploded with exasperation. "Do you think *I* knew what to do?"

Janet put her hand on his arm. "Sebastian..."

"When I got off that plane," said Sebastian, ignoring her, "all I could think of was that the only time you came to see me in the States you refused to take me to Disneyland. I was six years old, Dad. Why wouldn't you take me to Disneyland, like other kids' dads do?"

There was a silence, during which Sebastian drew his palm down his upper lip. He didn't take his eyes off his father's face, though.

"I thought it was a load of nonsense," said Frank eventually, the lines on his forehead deepening. "And I still do, if you want the truth. Grown men dancing around in Mickey Mouse costumes!"

"But I was *six*," protested Sebastian. Then his face changed, and he looked at his father as if an ancient question had been answered. "You don't understand much about kids, do you?"

Frank's moustache twitched. He gave

Sebastian a complacent look, which Annabel recognized from the many times Sebastian had turned it on her. He spread his hands. "What practice have I had?"

Sebastian's mouth relaxed, not quite into a smile, but into calmness. "Well, you have the perfect opportunity now, sir," he said. "You can practise on Annabel."

They all looked at her. Annabel, who knew the garland round her head made her look as sickly-sweet as a Victorian greetings card, concentrated on not blushing. "You'd better watch out," said Sebastian to Frank, though his eyes were on Annabel. "She'll be making a sculpture of *you* next!"

Frank and Janet laughed, but Annabel's lack of breath wouldn't allow her to join in. Sebastian was still looking at her. She couldn't look at him.

"Come on, Missus," said Frank, patting Janet's hand. He got up and shook out his trouser-bottoms. "Are we having a wedding today, or not?"

To Annabel's astonishment, Janet reached over and kissed Sebastian on the cheek. "You're a good boy, Sebastian," she murmured. Then she turned to Annabel. "And as for you, young lady ... well, we're all so proud of you!"

Annabel was proud, too. She wanted to smile, but her throat was gripped by the threat

203

of tears, and her face-muscles wouldn't move. She nodded and blinked, and hoped her mother would understand.

Janet stood up, smiling broadly. "Now, Maid of Honour, bring me my bridal bouquet. And where are the gentlemen's buttonholes? How dare you neglect your duties!"

Annabel got to her feet so fast that the rocking chair was still rocking when she reached the door. She picked up her stiff skirts and ran into the kitchen. If my heart were a horse, she thought, it would have won every steeplechase in the racing calendar by now, and made me a fortune.

A DIFFERENT
KIND OF LOVE

During the wedding ceremony Annabel was too nervous to look at anything except Janet's lacy back and Frank's dark grey one. At the reception she concentrated on her plate, eating little, conscious that rose petals were falling down the neck of her dress as the garland wilted in the heat. By the time the dancing started she was sure every bridge between her old and new lives had been burnt, leaving her stranded.

"Annabel!" Lucy rushed up to her and slid to a halt. She was wearing an orangey-tan dress with thin shoulder straps. Some of her curls had escaped from the gilt clips above her ears. She looked nerve-wrackingly pretty. "Come and dance."

She pulled Annabel's hand, but Annabel resisted. "Who with?"

"With anyone who asks you. Come *on*, will

you? There are loads of students here, from Janet's university. One or two of them are talent. Honestly."

Annabel didn't move. "Lucy, they're not interested in fifteen-year-olds," she said reasonably. "Even the smelly anoraky ones aren't that desperate."

"Well, that's just where you're wrong." She grabbed Annabel's arm, pulling her close. "You see that one in the cream jacket?"

"I thought he was a waiter."

"Oh, Annabel! He's asked me to dance. He's in his second year, doing history."

"And what did you tell him you're doing? Not GCSEs, I bet."

Lucy went very red. "A levels."

"You told him you're *eighteen*?" This was bold, even for Lucy.

"Well, seventeen."

Annabel couldn't help laughing. "Go on, then, dance with him. Remember your parents are here, though!"

"Aren't you coming?"

She shook her head. More petals dropped from her head-dress. "I'm not even sure I *can* dance in all these petticoats, even if I wanted to."

Lucy shrugged, letting go of her arm. Annabel watched her orangey-tan figure skirt the dancefloor and join the group which contained the cream jacket. He was fairish, medium built, with an eager, little-boy expression. Hardly *talent*.

Her gaze began a slow wander around the room. Varying amounts of alcohol had influenced everyone, it seemed. Janet was at the flushed, talkative, tripping-over-her-dress stage. Frank looked more relaxed than Annabel had ever seen him, lounging in a chair with his legs going in different directions, chuckling at some joke the landlord of the Rose and Crown was telling him, probably not for the first time. She sighed, and went on looking round the room.

Then she saw Sebastian.

He was standing with his head down and one knee bent, his shoulders and the sole of his shoe flat against the wall. Annabel had no recollection of speaking to him at the ceremony or the reception. When the band had struck up the opening number she'd seen him slip out of the ballroom. He must have re-entered it without her noticing.

She went to his side. "Where have you been?" she asked gently. "Are you all right?"

"Sure." He pushed himself off the wall with his foot. She noticed that he'd taken off his tie and loosened his collar. "I went outside for some air, that's all. It's like a Shanghai nightclub in here."

Annabel, who had never been to a nightclub, in Shanghai or anywhere else, glanced curiously at his face. It was its usual neat-featured self, except that the skin on it looked stretched, and the muscles underneath tense. Around his eyes there were definite signs of strain. One way and another, it had been a long day.

"Have you had some champagne?" he asked.

"No."

"Don't you like it?" His lips began a smile. Annabel wished for the hundredth time that she was older, taller, browner, more sophisticated. More Californian, somehow.

"I don't know. I've never tasted it."

"Really? Never?"

"Janet doesn't exactly keep a case of it in the cellar, you know."

"Well, she should. C'mon, let's go find some."

She followed him to the table where waiters were dispensing soft drinks, beer and leftover champagne. Sebastian secured two glasses, one fuller than the other. "*Salud*, as we say in Mexico," he said, handing her the fuller one.

"I can't drink all this!"

"Wait till you try it." He took a sip of his. "Go on, Little Bo Peep."

She raised her glass. The bubbles burst stickily on her nose. She sipped the champagne. It tasted like sour lemonade.

"That's it," said Sebastian, gesturing with his glass. "Take a gulp."

"Are you trying to get Little Bo Peep drunk?"

The tension in his face began to disperse. Annabel sipped the champagne again. Perhaps, after some practice, she might like it. There were worse things in life than sour lemonade.

"Dance?" He finished his own champagne and put the glass down. "Drink the rest of yours, or someone'll steal it."

As they picked their way between the tables, avoiding abandoned handbags and trampled pieces of wedding cake, Annabel was reminded of how she'd felt when she'd followed him into the buttercup field. Frightened, but reckless. Drinking the champagne so quickly had set off little rockets in her brain. Under the taffeta petticoats, her legs shook.

The music was medium tempo wedding-party music. Older men steered their partners importantly round the floor, and people of Janet and Frank's age shuffled with their arms around each other or jigged hand-in-hand with children. Annabel and Sebastian would have to dance together, or not at all.

He picked up her hand nonchalantly, like something he'd just found lying around, and tugged her towards him. At the moment she was about to collide with his chest he dropped her hand, put his arm around her waist and picked up her other hand. It felt peculiar to be handled so expertly, as if she were his tennis racquet.

"You've done this before, haven't you?" she said.

"Haven't *you*?" Sebastian put his mouth close to her ear. His breath felt damp. "Relax, will you? Get nearer me, for a start."

Annabel was glad of the stiff bodice and three petticoats. She was glad she was wearing a garland of thorny roses around her head. Even so, Sebastian's body felt very close indeed. She could discern the different landscapes of chest, stomach, pelvis, legs. His palm pressed the small of her back so firmly it was impossible to push him away. Her nose was close enough to the pink rose in his buttonhole for her to smell it. Undeterred by the thorns, he rested his chin on her temple, breathing fast.

Her heart felt squashed and uncomfortable. Something apart from the blue silk sash restricted her breath. Incredible as it was, the boy she'd looked at so closely and for so long – close enough to draw him, close enough to sculpt a roughly recognizable likeness – was actually enjoying being close to *her*. It was a revelation.

"You're pretty good at this," said Sebastian, his voice resonating through her skull. "You haven't trodden on my feet once. And your knees are so low they don't collide with mine at all."

"Are you calling me a dwarf?"

"More like Snow White, in that dress." He moved his face away from hers and grinned. "But you look nice in it, you know. It suits you."

Annabel knew this wasn't true. "It doesn't. It wouldn't suit anyone. Even Snow White looked daft in hers."

"Nonsense!" She liked the way he said "non-sense", making it into two words. Her accent sounded so zipped-up in comparison. "You know perfectly well that every guy in Broughton would be here dancing with you if he could."

This was so ridiculous Annabel started to giggle. "*What* guys?" she asked. "Don't you know there are no boys in Broughton? Or at least there weren't until ... er..."

"Annabel, what is it with you? When are you going to stop *dreaming*?"

He'd stopped dancing. He stood with his arm still encircling her back, staring at her. He looked like the sculpture. His head was tilted, and the open collar of his shirt exposed some of the neck she'd laboured so painfully to reproduce. After all their experiences together, Annabel had thought he was getting to know her. But what he'd just said revealed her to be mistaken.

"I don't understand what you mean," she

said truthfully. "I'm not dreaming. I just don't think people want to dance with ... with girls like me, that's all."

They started to dance again. But Annabel's body felt cumbersome, and she kept losing time with the music.

"Why the hell not?" Sebastian was almost scolding her, though she didn't know what she'd done wrong. "At my High School they'd be lining up."

Annabel's heart seemed to fill her chest, leaving no room for her lungs. She was sure Sebastian would notice the curved neckline of her dress bumping up and down. Was he trying to say something to her without quite saying it?

Or had the moment come when *she* must say something to *him*?

"But I don't want anyone else," she half-whispered, half-hoping he wouldn't hear. "I only want *you*."

The music stopped. All around them dancers stood still and applauded. Taking Annabel's elbow, Sebastian led her to the side of the dancefloor. He sat down on a little gilt chair. He looked worried. "You already have me, Annabel. I'm right here."

"But you're my *stepbrother*!" She was racked by a strong desire to scream. This wasn't supposed to happen. Why hadn't Sebastian reacted in the way she'd rehearsed

212

so many times? She swayed against the table. "Why are you teasing me? Because I'm your little sister? Or just because you don't like me?"

He was hurt. There, leaning on a stained tablecloth in a stuffy ballroom, Annabel realized for the first time in her life that she had genuinely hurt a boy.

"Of course I like you, Annabel." His eyes were full of dismay. He put his elbows on the table and lowered his head into his hands. "God, I'm just so *tired*. I don't know what's going on any more."

Annabel sat down too. Every pleasure and pain Sebastian had ever given her collected in her heart. "I'm sorry," she said. "I'm so sorry, really. It was stupid of me to say that. And I didn't mean it, anyway."

He took his head out of his hands and looked at her. His eyes were very dark. Clearly, the moment *had* come. Annabel knew that the only thing which might stop the words coming out would be a natural disaster or a terrorist attack, and it had to happen right now, this second.

"I know you like me. But I want you to love me. And that's impossible."

He looked puzzled. Then his face wiped itself clean of all expression. His wide-open eyes had never looked so wide-open. "But I *do* love you!"

Annabel couldn't stop herself gasping.

"And I don't mean like a brother or anything." He leaned towards her. "Listen. I've met a lot of psychiatrists and professors, and my friend Phil's mother's a screen-writer in Hollywood, which is pretty impressive. But I've never met a *sculptor* before. You're really, really special. Don't you know that? You're bright, and sensitive, and gifted with an incredible talent. I envy you, Annabel. I mean, what can *I* do? Hot-shot my way around a tennis court? Big deal!"

Annabel gasped again.

"When I first met you, I thought you seemed ... well, younger than you are." He beat his palm gently on the tablecloth, warming to his theme. "It wasn't ignorance or stupidity. It wasn't even innocence, really. It was just that you hadn't learned the rules, somehow."

Unlike Lucy, he means, thought Annabel.

He reached across the table for her hand. She let him take it. "But watching you make that sculpture was fantastic," he said. "You treat your talent as if it's your God-given right to have it. You act like – like a princess or something, expecting the best from everyone, and doing *your* best all the time. And dammit, Annabel, aside from anything else, you're more beautiful than any princess I've ever seen."

Annabel couldn't speak, but she managed

not to gasp.

"While I was watching you I realized that talent and beauty are parts of the same thing," he explained. "I'd noticed before that you were pretty – who wouldn't? But a perfect-looking girl who can't *do* anything is just a ... a..."

"A Barbie-Brain?"

He squeezed her hand. "You understand, don't you? I didn't know how I felt until I saw you making that horse out of stones. It's more than I've ever felt for a girl before, but it has nothing to do with getting romantic and exchanging rings and all that stuff. It's just a different kind of love."

Annabel looked at the tablecloth, immobilized with astonishment. Who would have thought such happiness could come from such an unexpected source? Sebastian had understood exactly the same thing about her as she had about him.

She glanced up at him. "You're quite right about the outside and the inside of a person being the same thing, you know. Frank saw it too, didn't he?"

A line, so thin she almost didn't notice it, appeared between his eyebrows. "What do you mean?"

"Well, something about the sculpture – just the way you were holding your head, or the shape of your eye socket or something, made

215

Frank think about not only you, but your mother," she explained. "That's what sculpture does, you see. It has a secret life of its own. Haven't you ever wondered if statues dance around when no one's looking at them?"

Sebastian stared at her.

"When I made the stone horse I realized that I was creating the *presence* of a horse, and I created the presence of your mother in the sculpture. Though neither of them exist in reality, both she and the horse are sort of – real, aren't they?"

Sebastian was still staring at her. He understood, though.

"Your father *does* love you," she assured him. "He sees how wrong he was to think he'd better forget you. And Janet always knew he was wrong, which was why she suggested you come to Broughton in the first place. She might be as predictable as a Mars bar, but she's not as stupid as one, you know. It was only when Frank looked at the sculpture that he saw the truth, though." At last, she found the courage to talk American. "Honey, that's *weird*!"

He threw back his head and laughed. Several heads turned, and turned away again tolerantly. "Every darned thing about this summer has been weird, Annabel. I'll remember it for the rest of my life."

"So will I." She gave him a deliberately pretty smile. The kind of smile she'd practised in the bathroom so many times. "Would you like a photograph? To take back to America with you?"

"A picture of *you*, do you mean?"

She nodded, feeling self-conscious. He looked at her with his head on one side. "Sure." He tilted his head the other way, like someone in an art gallery examining a painting. "In those washed-out jeans and that little blue and white shirt?"

"If you like," she said, pleased but mildly astonished. "Er ... I didn't know you'd noticed what I wear, though."

He smiled. "There's a whole lot of stuff you don't know, Annabel. Do you think I've been going around with my eyes shut for the past five weeks?"

Annabel didn't know what she thought. When Sebastian first arrived, all she'd wanted was for him to think her prettier than Lucy, and put her photograph in his wallet. But the stone horse had made him see beyond her prettiness, to the place where the real Annabel Bairstow acted out her dreams. Janet was right about that, too. Being pretty wasn't enough.

"Let's go get some drinks," he suggested, "before the music starts again." He stood up and scanned the crowd. "I'll ask Lucy to dance, if I can get her away from that funny-looking guy in the white tux."

The band began a faster, louder number.

Annabel got up to follow Sebastian to the bar, but was stopped by a masculine hand on her arm. "Can you dance in that dress?" asked Sean, bending his head close to hers.

As he straightened up she looked at him. He had his Milky Bar face on, soft and freckle-smudged. His eyes had the dreamy look of someone unaccustomed to champagne. His hair, recently washed, flopped over his fore-head. The sight of the dimple beside his mouth summoned every emotion Annabel had experienced on this emotional day, and before she knew what she was doing she'd put her arms around his neck. "Just try and stop me," she said.

She was too close to see his expression clearly, but if he was surprised she didn't care. She saw his mouth open a little, as if to speak, but he didn't speak. Instead, he kissed her.

She had never imagined a boy's lips could be so pliable yet so purposeful. Her teeth didn't get in the way, and she didn't strain her body away from his, as she usually did when half-drunk boys tried to kiss her. When they broke away from each other and she took her arms from round his neck, she thought she had never seen anyone look so – well, so *nice*.

"Sebastian's gone to get me a drink," she told him.

"Who?"

She grinned, and so did Sean. Then he took

218

her hand and led her to the middle of the dancefloor. Annabel pulled the garland out of her hair. She aimed it at a table, but it fell on the floor. And soon the other dancers had trampled on the few remaining rose petals, spoiling them for ever.

FISH FEET
Veronica Bennett

Erik Shaw loves dancing and wants to audition for the Royal Ballet School. But that means making some tough decisions – such as giving up the Falcons football team and letting down old friends. Then there's Ruth, a fellow ballet dancer to whom Erik is becoming increasingly attracted. Can their relationship survive the rigours of practice and competition? And has Erik got the strength of will as well as the talent to achieve his goal?

MONKEY
Veronica Bennett

By teenager Harry Pritchard's own admission, he's a dork.

At school he's bullied by the vicious "Brig" Fox; at home he's weighed down by the chores his mother sets him. When she volunteers him to visit a patient of hers, Simon Schofield, it seems like the final straw. She says it'll do him good, but how can it help him end Brig's bullying? Or get a part in the Drama Club play? Or win the attentions of Louise Harding, the girl of his dreams? After meeting Simon, though, Harry's life undergoes some dramatic – and traumatic – changes!